Luke's first impulse was to get out of the cabin.

His upbringing had been rough, and he'd never held relationships in high esteem. Now he faced a bigger emotional upheaval in the form of one small, curvy woman.

Miranda shook him to his core, rocking beliefs he'd held for a lifetime, because her innocence was real. She understood what honor was and that once the code was broken you could never go back.

His gaze landed on the wrought-iron bedstead in the corner of the room. The desire that had been his constant companion since their embrace the other night hit him hard. Hell, who was he kidding? He'd wanted her ever since he'd seen her.

Dear Reader,

This month, Silhouette Desire is celebrating milestones, miniseries—and, of course, sensual, emotional and compelling love stories. Every book is a treasured keeper in Lass Small's miniseries THE KEEPERS OF TEXAS, but this month, the continuation of this wonderful series about the Keeper family marks a milestone for Lass—the publication of her 50th book for Silhouette with *The Lone Texan,* also our MAN OF THE MONTH selection!

Desire is also proud to present the launch of two brand-new miniseries. First, let us introduce you to THE RULEBREAKERS, Leanne Banks's fabulous new series about three strong and sexy heroes. Book one is *Millionaire Dad*—and it's a story you won't want to miss. Next, meet the first of a few good men and women in uniform in the passion-filled new series BACHELOR BATTALION, by Maureen Child. The first installment, *The Littlest Marine,* will utterly delight you.

Continuing this month is the next book in Peggy Moreland's series TEXAS BRIDES about the captivating McCloud sisters, *A Sparkle in the Cowboy's Eyes.* And rounding out the month are two wonderful novels—*Miranda's Outlaw* by Katherine Garbera, and *The Texas Ranger and the Tempting Twin* by Pamela Ingrahm.

I hope you enjoy all six of Silhouette Desire's love stories this month—and every month.

Regards,

Melissa Senate

Melissa Senate
Senior Editor Silhouette Books

Please address questions and book requests to:
Silhouette Reader Service
U.S.: 3010 Walden Ave., P.O. Box 1325, Buffalo, NY 14269
Canadian: P.O. Box 609, Fort Erie, Ont. L2A 5X3

KATHERINE GARBERA

MIRANDA'S OUTLAW

SILHOUETTE *Desire*

Published by Silhouette Books

America's Publisher of Contemporary Romance

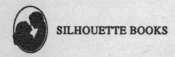

SILHOUETTE BOOKS

ISBN 0-373-76169-4

MIRANDA'S OUTLAW

Books by Katherine Garbera

Silhouette Desire

The Bachelor Next Door #1104
Miranda's Outlaw #1169

KATHERINE GARBERA

Interpersonal relationships have always fascinated Katherine Garbera, and writing romance gives her a chance to explore those relationships. She wrote her first novel to prove to herself she could do it, and was hooked on writing. A longtime reader of romance, she is addicted to happy endings. Her personal life has been like a romance novel. She met her husband, Matt, in Fantasyland at Walt Disney World and has two wonderful children, Courtney and Lucas. Katherine is a member of Romance Writers of America, and is the past winner of the Georgia Romance Writers Maggie Award. Her hobbies include reading, shopping, playing the flute and counted cross-stitch. She's always believed that everything she dreams she can do. In a world so technologically advanced, Katherine believes we need more romance in our daily lives and hopes to create that with her novels. She loves to hear from readers. You can write to her at: P.O. Box 1806, Davenport, FL 33836.

To Charlotte and David Smith, my mom and dad, who raised me to believe that I could do anything I put my mind to and then encouraged and supported me when I tried things that were beyond my skills. Without your guidance and love I don't think I'd be who I am today. Thank you.

Acknowledgements

Special thanks to Tanja Lammers, who took time out of her busy schedule to proofread my manuscript and check it for a North Carolina feeling.

Also my appreciation to Sandra Diaz, USAFR, Aeromedical Evacuation Technician, who answered my endless questions on medical procedures and told me the way things really worked when I said "What if...?"

And lastly, thanks to my dear friend Carol Quinto, who encouraged me to keep writing after that first rejection letter and gave selflessly of her knowledge when I had no answers and too many questions. Your laughter, friendship and warm generosity will be with me forever.

One

Miranda Colby coaxed her Mercedes off the road, knowing the valiant little car wouldn't go another inch.

The rough mountain trail looked like an ad for *Adventurers* magazine. Potholes and muddy patches lined the road like stains on a wedding-ring quilt, making what had once probably been a passable road into a quagmire.

She knew the cabin had to be close by. Determined to reach its shelter before the storm broke, she stepped out of the car and felt the world sink.

Clutching the roof of her car, she pried her left foot out of the muck. She balanced herself on a patch of grass and pulled her right foot out of the mud. The mate to her now-ugly shoe hadn't made the journey.

Miranda bit back a sigh of disgust, rummaging around in the back seat of the car until she found her worn canvas boat shoes. As she slid them on, she glanced at the sky.

Ominous black clouds threatened, and a roll of thunder

echoed through the valley. A chance to learn how to survive in the "real" world was what she needed.

But even a city girl could tell the display would turn into a full-fledged downpour with very little urging. Grabbing the groceries and her purse, she locked the doors to her car.

The directions from the rental agent had been vague, but she knew that her cabin was located near the summit of this mountain. With that in mind, she forged ahead until she reached a dirt path.

The late-afternoon wind whipped through the trees. Miranda held the sack of groceries a bit tighter to her chest and quickened her pace. A few more minutes, then she'd be at the rental cabin. She promised herself a long, hot bath, a cup of steaming Earl Grey tea and a whole bag of Oroes.

Reaching a crossroads on the path, she froze. The sound of a man's voice singing a ballad about lost love carried clearly in the mountain air. The haunting melody and achingly sad words touched a part of her she'd locked away long ago. Surprised for a moment, she listened to the rich baritone that drifted with the wind through the trees.

Where was he? she wondered. Her rental agent had promised seclusion, and civilization was several miles away. Whoever the man was, he'd have to be singing pretty loudly for her to hear him unless...

She was lost.

Miranda groaned out loud.

She rounded a curve in the lane and stopped as a two-story glass-and-cedar structure loomed into view. It fit the landscape perfectly, blending with nature to make the house appear almost as if it were part of the mountain.

The singing stopped, followed by a loud splash. She followed the sounds around to the back of the house. Miranda scanned the shadowed area on the rear porch. A mountain of white frothy bubbles covered the entire surface of an old-fashioned claw-foot bathtub. The foamy spray beckoned her weary body closer and Miranda fought the urge to strip off her clothes and dive into the inviting water. Of course, she'd never do such a thing.

She shivered again as the breeze kicked up. She took an involuntary step closer. Now she could see the steam rising from the tub, and it looked appealing in the chilly weather. A warm oasis, she thought.

Miranda sighed. It had been a grueling week at the office—the end of tax season always left her exhausted—but this year it was more than just the work. She was tired, tired of her friends, tired of her life-style, tired of seeing her ex-fiancé and his new family everywhere she went.

She'd poured her life into her career, awakening one morning to find that something was missing. She'd handed in her resignation, but Mark didn't believe her. He'd told her to take a leave of absence, and he'd hold her job for her. The offer was flattering, but she'd warned him she might not come back. Mark had only laughed. He said she belonged in high-level finance. She was too bright and too competitive to stay away for long.

Was she? Miranda had her doubts. Right now she wanted only peace and quiet. Right now she'd settle for climbing in that steaming tub, and soaking away the aches in her body and soul—but she doubted if Mountain Lake Lodge's hospitality extended to a steam bath in an old-fashioned tub.

The setting sun fought through the gathering storm clouds to cast long shadows on the grass and wildflowers that blanketed the lawn. She stood at the back of some stranger's cabin and knew she'd followed the wrong directions. Murphy's Law strikes again, she thought wryly.

As Miranda watched, the bubbles parted and a head and torso emerged amid a spray of steam and foam. She stared at the strongly muscled back. An intricately drawn tattoo of a bird—some kind of hawk, she thought—glistened on one shoulder as the man continued to emerge from the heated water. The complex design made the predatory bird seem real. She felt its intense gaze on her almost as if the bird stared at her. Her fingers tingled with the need to trace the hawk and the male flesh beneath it.

She cleared her throat hoping to catch the man's attention, but the sound died before it reached her lips.

The man shook his head flinging soap and water everywhere. He stretched his arms toward the sky, an outward reaching as if he were welcoming the coming storm. Miranda felt more of an intruder than ever.

He tilted his head back and let out a loud rebel yell. The kind that men had issued for ages when they were staking a claim or acknowledging the primal male buried inside the more civilized one.

Long midnight-colored strands of hair brushed the top of his shoulders. He combed through the wet locks with his fingers, revealing a diamond stud earring in one lobe.

A battered Stetson sat next to the tub along with a lit cigar. The surrounding wood deck was bare except for those items and a small pile of clothing. She wondered why she hadn't noticed it before. Smoke drifted upward in a lazy spiral, merging with the clouds of steam. The Hawk, for that was how she thought of him, picked up the hat and settled it low on his forehead as he leaned back against the foot of the tub.

She'd never seen a person more at home in the outdoor environment. She couldn't picture herself sitting outside in broad daylight—naked. Apparently this man had very little modesty and more ease with his own nudity than she did.

Miranda tried again to say *something,* to alert him to her presence, but she was too fascinated by the sight of him. She closed her eyes and counted to ten, sure that she imagined the man, the bath and the bird. He was still there when she opened her eyes.

He lifted the smoking cigar and took a long drag on it. She wrinkled her nose at the pungent scent of the tobacco.

Definitely a real person—the acrid smell couldn't be part of anyone's imagination.

Before she could move he began singing again, but this tune hardly resembled the haunting song she'd heard earlier. The words were embarrassing and colorfully blunt.

A blush heated her face, and, despite the situation, she smiled. For years she'd accepted what passed as sophisticated boardroom humor among her male colleagues. She'd never found their sexual innuendoes embarrassing—just annoying. But this man, the Hawk, with his very crudeness, his earthiness, stirred deep feelings within her and shook her to her mud-splattered toes.

Too embarrassed to stay and ask directions, Miranda decided that she'd take her chances with the approaching storm. She pivoted on her heel, prepared to leave without alerting the man to her presence. A small rock caught under her shoe and rolled. Her feet slid out from under her as the bag of groceries went flying. Miranda let out an inelegant shriek. Her backside hit the hard ground. The Hawk rose from the tub.

"Stop!" she yelled, and covered her face with her hands on the off chance that he didn't heed her warning. She didn't want to deal with all that naked masculinity. A three-piece suit she could handle, but not this.

"You okay, darlin'?" he asked from the porch. That lazy, deep voice brushed across her senses like the spring breezes across winter's icy embrace, releasing a flood of longings that she thought she'd buried.

She said nothing, only pulled her knees to her chest and hid her face against them. She felt the need to cry, to laugh, to rail against a merciless God who would send her to the one person she couldn't ask for help. A man who spoke with a deep Texan drawl and probably knew these mountains like the back of his hand. A man who made her thoughts scatter like leaves in a windstorm. A man, she thought as she heard him approach, who was standing next to her, naked and dripping wet. She sighed, biting back the hysterical laughter that she felt bubbling up in her stomach.

A large, rough hand touched her shoulder. "Are you okay?"

Keeping her face covered, Miranda said, "No—I mean yes. Yes, I'm fine." She wanted to stand but couldn't unless she uncovered her face. "Are you decent?"

"I've got clothes on," he said with a deep, rich chuckle that filled the meadow with its sound. Cautiously she peered through her fingers, grateful that he now wore the jeans that had been a dark puddle on the wooden porch only moments before. She sighed in relief.

His bare chest was still wet and small droplets of water clung to the matted hair. A longing welled up inside of her to touch his damp chest. She knew she was staring but somehow couldn't stop. Miranda shook herself out of the trance this man seemed to have cast over her. She wasn't a woman ruled by impulses, especially irrational ones, she reminded herself.

Reaching down to clasp her arm above the elbow, he hauled her to her feet. "What are you doing on my property?"

"I'm lost."

She stared into eyes the color of chocolate. Despite the grin on his face, his expression wasn't welcoming and warm, but filled instead with a desolation that her soul recognized. Part of her wanted to reach out to someone whose wounds were as deep as hers, but common sense told her to keep her distance. How could this tall, lean mountain man have anything in common with her?

He stared at her for so long that Miranda was afraid she'd ripped her clothing in the fall or rubbed dirt on her face during the long trek to his cabin. She brushed her hand across her cheeks and nose before trying to tame her wild mane into something that looked normal, less like a Halloween wig.

"Oh, darlin', I think I'm the one lost."

His gentle smile and playful wink caught her off guard. The words dripped over her like honey on a warm biscuit. Tempting, sweet promises she'd regret believing later.

Despite her predicament, she smiled at him before realizing what she was doing. Country charm beat city sophistication any day. She shrugged the thought aside and gathered her senses as best she could.

"I've rented a cabin near here from the Mountain Lake Lodge. Can you direct me to it?" Her gourmet groceries were scattered across the lawn looking as out of place as she felt. Miranda gathered them quickly. The paper sack torn beyond repair, she glanced around helplessly.

"I'll go one better and take you there." He walked back to the porch. His long-legged stride captured her attention. She stared against her better judgment as he sat down on the wood deck. Sticking his cigar in his mouth, he pulled on battered cowboy boots. "I've got some extra brown bags. I'll get one for you."

Miranda watched him disappear inside the cabin. He looked as though he'd be more at home riding the range than in the mountains of North Carolina. Still he seemed to fit in here as if he were sure of the environment and his place in it.

"Where's your car?" he asked when he came back with the bags. A faded denim shirt now covered the tattoo, but allowed her to glimpse the muscles of his chest as he bent and picked up a few of the scattered items on the ground.

She wondered what his hard flesh would feel like beneath her fingers or pressed against her breasts. *Get a grip, Miranda. He's a stranger.*

"Down the hill. I didn't realize the incline would be so steep." She glanced quickly at her groceries trying to ascertain that nothing embarrassing had been in the bag.

"I'll take you back to get the car first." He passed a box

of chocolate-covered biscotti and gourmet espresso beans to her.

"You don't have to," she said, hating to be dependent on anyone—especially a man. They always expected something in return. She shoved the items into the brown bag without looking at them. "Just point me in the right direction and I'll be fine."

He took the cigar from his mouth and she watched the smoke as he exhaled. She was fascinated by the spiral and his obvious enjoyment of the tobacco product. The pungent smell didn't bother her at all, she realized.

"I don't mind taking you," he said. The expression on his face was determined.

Miranda knew that he planned to help her whether she wanted him along or not. She was annoyed by his assumption that she needed his help—but the challenge in those chocolate brown eyes persuaded her to hold her temper. She doubted many people got the better of this man, and after the trials she'd been through today, she didn't have the heart for a battle.

"This mountain is dangerous, darlin'," he said as though reading her thoughts. "Especially to inexperienced vacationers. Besides, the sooner I get you to your cabin the sooner you'll be out of my hair. No offense, ma'am, but I like my privacy."

Miranda didn't bother to correct his impression that she was on vacation. Let him think what he wanted. Hopefully after today they wouldn't see each other again. She made a mental note to send him a box of cigars, and replied stiffly, "Thank you. If you're determined to act as a guide, can we leave? I don't want to get caught in this storm."

"Sure thing, darlin'."

Working quickly they gathered up the rest of her groceries and Miranda tossed them into the sack. She tried to ignore the fact that the man's jeans clung to his body like a second skin. Tried to ignore that the brush of his fingers against the back of her hand kindled an awareness she'd never experienced before. Tried to ignore that her body recognized in him something her mind wouldn't accept.

Thunder rumbled and streaks of distant lightning filled the sky. Miranda shivered in response. She was in trouble, even if he helped her back to the car and gave her directions. If the Mercedes had cooled enough to start, she'd still never make it to the cabin without getting drenched.

"That lightning's still far off, darlin'. We'll make it to your car."

"My name's Miranda Colby," she said coolly. She hated being called by a generic endearment like *darlin'*. She wanted to be polite to him because he was going out of his way to help her but she resented his condescending tone.

"Luke Romero," he said extending one large hand to her. The skin on his palm felt rough against her own and she involuntarily tightened her fingers. Slowly she released his hand, hating to lose the warmth, the security offered by that brief polite action. His hands were strong, capable. Not like the soft, well-manicured hands she was accustomed to shaking.

"We better get going if we're going to beat the rain," he said, and walked around the house. He stubbed the cigar out and put the stump in his shirt pocket. Miranda followed quickly, ready to find a warm, comfortable place.

Luke stashed her grocery bag in the back seat of his Suburban and helped Miranda into the truck. The courtesy was one that he usually didn't bother with, but this lady looked tired. She smiled her thanks, but lines of strain bracketed her mouth, and he sensed she didn't want his company.

He suspected her tiredness went beyond the fatigue of a long car drive or overwork. She had an air of vulnerability about her that was at odds with the elegance of her appearance. Bruised, he thought, as though even her bones ached. Shapely bones, his libido reminded him, as he walked around the truck.

Miss Colby was stacked. Though he'd sworn off women, he couldn't help noticing the way her silk T-shirt clung to her generous curves and her designer jeans molded over rounded hips that invited a man's touch. His palm actually tingled with the need to pat her backside.

Suddenly Luke was glad that the woman had the good sense to be leery of him. He didn't want to play the games that women inevitably played with men. He'd moved to the mountains to escape all of that.

Luke downshifted the Suburban as he navigated the twisting dirt road. Maybe, he thought, she was just embarrassed at needing someone's help. A lot of women these days liked to think they were self-sufficient. Whatever the reason, it was none of his business. He'd come to the mountains, not to play the knight to some damsel in distress, but to rid himself of the stress and temptation in the city. To find a place where he was content and at peace.

He drove in silence, the tension in the truck simmering between them, like a live wire downed in an electrical storm.

He rounded the bend and saw a battered green sports car parked on the side of the road. Mud from last night's rain caked the wheels. Luke bit back an instinctive curse and slowed the Suburban. "That your car?"

"Yes," she said softly, not meeting his gaze. "I had no idea the mountain would be..."

"So steep," he finished for her. He wished old Edgar would give up trying to make money off his hunting cabin. Without fail, he rented his place to someone with no camping experience. Luke's first impulse was to tow her car down the mountain to the fork leading to her place, so that she'd be out of his hair. But last night's mud and the threatening storm worked against him. He knew her car wouldn't make it, even with the Suburban doing all the work.

Well, hell, he thought. This is what came of being neighborly. He backed the truck up to the Mercedes and got out to attach the chain to the car. Rain started to fall, not a soft summer rain, but a harsh torrent. He stood there for a minute, sure that the Almighty was punishing him for his earlier thoughts about the woman. He'd had no right to think of her in purely sexual terms and now he was paying the price.

He attached the chain to the back of his truck before climbing into the cab. Cold drops trickled slowly down his neck. The earthy scent of rain mingled with the essence of Miranda Colby. The primitive scents teased his base instincts and he reacted like a man who'd forgotten. Forgotten that cold rain could lead to cuddling. Forgotten that cuddling could lead to bold caresses. Forgotten the soft feel of that one special woman in his arms.

Miranda stared at him—guilt pouring off her like the icy drops from saturated clouds. Desire hit him hard. He knew he could never have her for his own but that didn't change the fact that he wanted her.

In spite of the fact that she was prickly—hell, that was part of the attraction.

Oh, damn, he thought, I've been too long without a woman.

He didn't say anything, or even look at her. Rain always made him irritable. It wasn't her fault he'd given in to the unusual chivalrous impulse to help her.

"I'm sorry you got wet," she said quietly. The tone in her voice clearly stated that she hadn't asked for his help.

He nodded in acknowledgment, but kept silent. After stepping carefully on the gas, Luke watched through the rearview mirror as her car lurched drunkenly out of the mud. It bounced on the rutted dirt like a pull toy in the hands of a giant.

He breathed deeply, trying to absorb the essence of her into the fabric of his being. There was something pure and

innocent about the woman sitting next to him, despite her
city sophistication. She didn't have the tough veneer he'd
encountered in city women before. He'd known more than
his share of hardened independent women who wanted only
one thing from a man. And while he had no doubt that this
little lady was successful, he knew there was much of life
she hadn't experienced. Part of his jaded soul was challenged by that innocence. He'd almost forgotten what innocence felt like. He quelled the urge to corrupt her.

She didn't look like someone who'd want to be isolated
on a mountain. She had the sleek polish of a professional
career woman. The humidity had caused her thick hair to
curl around her face in a way that brought to mind pixies.
But he knew the cut would fall into a sophisticated style
just as easily.

Forcing his attention off Miranda, he eased slowly forward, gathering the speed needed to tow the car up the
mountain. The Suburban could tow twice the weight, but
her car had him worried. The body and wheelbase were
battered from driving up the mountain. Frankly, he was
surprised she'd made it as far as she had. It said something
about her determination.

"Please, stop."

Startled, Luke braked and glanced at her, arching one
brow in question.

"I'd rather go to my rental cabin."

"Darlin', your cabin is on the other side of the mountain.
You're only about twenty minutes' walking distance in this
weather, but you're about two hours in driving time."

"I'll be on my way then. Thanks."

She had the door open before her words registered. Stepping out into the pouring rain, she reached back for her
food. "Give me a minute to stash this in the Mercedes—"

"There's no way that car will make it down the side of
this mountain and back up the other. I'll let you try it if

you're determined. But I'm not going to haul you out of the mud again until the storm lets up."

The stubborn tilt of her jaw told him he'd made a mistake. His words had been taken as a challenge instead of fact. He bet she never turned down a dare. "Darlin', it's the car, not you."

She just stood there making him feel big and mean in a way he hadn't since Brett looked up at him with big weepy eyes and asked why Luke wasn't his daddy anymore.

"I can't stay with you," she said, her voice heavy with raw emotion.

"I'm not asking you to move in, darlin', but you can stay at my cabin until the rain clears."

She hesitated, but she really had little choice. Reluctantly, she nodded, "Just until the rain lets up a bit then I'll walk over to the rental place."

The rain slowed to a steady downpour that Luke knew from experience would last until dawn. Though the storm wasn't an intense one, the ground would be slick and the night treacherous. Already the sky had darkened and in another twenty minutes it would be pitch-black outside.

He waited patiently for her to reseat herself and close the door. He refused to look at her but the image of her in that wet T-shirt stayed firmly in his mind. The image of her hardened nipples peaked against the cold, damp cloth wouldn't leave. *Would they be that responsive to his mouth and fingers?*

When she was settled, he put the truck back into motion. Damn fool woman. Hell, damn fool man for caring about her safety. The touch of vulnerability beneath her sophisticated facade made him want to protect her. Despite the lessons he'd learned about women from his ex-wife.

He couldn't let her go alone to Edgar's hunting cabin even though it was what he should do. The mountain and Mother Nature in general weren't kind to the weaker sex.

He knew some women were strong—stronger than him—but this little thing wasn't.

She looked as if a gust of wind could push her over the side of his mountain. She had no car, no coat and would probably insist on taking that bag of junk food with her. Luke shook his head and cursed his daddy for raising him with a strict code pertaining to women. Without that upbringing he'd probably let her go off on her own.

He pulled into his driveway and stared at the woman next to him. The woman whose pretty gray eyes reminded him of the mist that ringed the mountain most mornings. A keen intelligence gleamed in her gaze along with a trace of fear. Fear of him? he wondered.

He walked around to open her door but she was already standing on the ground when he got there. She had that bag of groceries clutched to her chest like a shield. Tugging the sack from her, he started for his house, letting her follow.

A damp chill settled over him as he led her to the front porch of the cabin he'd built with his own hands. Staring at it now—imagining how it looked to her eyes—he felt a sense of pride.

He knew from past experience that his house would be warm and dry. The last thing he wanted was to go back out into the wet night.

"It's cold and dark. The woods are dangerous to novice hikers. Stay with me until morning."

"I'd rather go on," she said. Something in that soft, tired voice convinced him to quit arguing with her. She needed to be at a place where she could relax. And it wasn't in a bachelor's cabin. Truth to tell, the sooner he left her presence the better it would be for him.

"Okay, I'll take you," he said. Her gaze melted under his, becoming so feminine that his gut tightened in reaction. "But under one condition."

"What?"

He wanted to reassure her but knew any protestations of

innocence from him wouldn't be convincing. He'd lived life to the fullest before retiring to the mountains. He stared into that fine-boned face and felt each of those decadent years as if they were wrapped around his neck with a heavy chain.

Years of recklessly prowling the country on his low rider with women of easy virtue. Years of barroom brawls and morning afters spent in the cool-down tank at the local sheriff's office. Years of fast living and hard times.

He smiled the grin that his ex-wife had told him would drive fear into the heart of the devil himself, and drawled in that deep Texan accent his daddy had taught him to use on a stubborn woman. "Darlin', it involves me, you and a warm, dry room."

Two

Miranda wrestled with the instinctive urge to bolt. The prospect of being lost in the woods seemed less frightening then being caught alone with this man. His sexy tempting grin, and soft drawling voice signaled trouble. Those chocolate-colored eyes saw right through her limited defenses.

"What?" she asked, stalling for time.

Her heart raced and her body sent fight-or-flight signals to her brain. *Calm down.* He's just a man. She bit back the hysterical laughter she felt welling in the back of her throat. He was so much more than *just a man.* And she knew it all the way to her guarded inner soul.

Using the composure she'd cultivated to use on the tough good-old-boy-network customers, she said, "I don't know what to say, Mr. Romero. I'm not..."

He silenced her with a long look, boldly roaming her face then traveling slowly all the way down her shivering body. The diamond stud in his ear winked at her, catching the fire from a jagged streak of lightning.

A crooked smile creased his face. Something changed in the air around her and in the intent in his eyes. What had frightened her earlier?

"I meant dinner, darlin'. Maybe some dry clothes. Nothing more."

His casual shrug made a mockery of her fear. Get a grip, she warned—he wasn't interested in anything more than getting her out of the storm. Stealing a glance at her sodden attire, she cringed. Wet cloth adhered to her skin like a die-cast mold, clinging to her body to reveal what she'd hoped to have hidden. She looked like the loser in a wet T-shirt contest.

"Okay," she said, hoping to sound more confident than she felt. Going toe-to-toe with a disgruntled business manager or arguing the finer points of tax laws she could handle. But on the basic man-to-woman interchanges, she was at a loss.

She wrapped her arms around her middle, feeling too exposed. Fatigue stole around her like cold on a winter's day, sapping her strength. What she really wanted was a bed to climb into and her comfortable sweats so that she'd be warm again. She wondered what it would be like if she stayed in the cabin with this warm, sexy man.

She cast a nervous glance in his direction. Luke stared out at the rain. It was obvious he'd already dismissed her from his mind. She wished he were as easily banished from *her* thoughts.

She'd never been *this* aware of a man before. No man had ever sparked a deep response in her. But Luke Romero was different. She wanted to know more about him. Why live on the top of a mountain? Why wear cowboy boots and a Stetson in a log cabin? Why help her though it was obvious he guarded his privacy?

His body heat radiated out to her in waves reminding her that it was still raining. She wanted to go closer to him and absorb his warmth into her tired body. She wanted to lean against him, to feel herself surrounded by him. *Wait a minute, Miranda.* No man who offered his support would want a woman who had nothing to give in return.

He opened the door, gesturing for her to step inside with a quick jerk of his head. *So much for country charm.*

She hesitated. Her mother had drilled into her at a very young age not to come into the house wet. "I'm soaked."

He glanced down, apparently noticing the puddle at his feet for the first time. He'd left his Stetson in the cab of his truck. The incongruity of a fully dressed man with wet hair probed her imagination.

"Close your eyes," he commanded. The man was obviously used to being in charge.

She gulped. Had he somehow peeked into her mind and read her lecherous thoughts. "Why?"

"I'm going to strip out of these wet clothes and go find something dry for us to wear."

I'm going to have a heart attack, she thought. She stared at him unsure of her own reactions. In a shaking voice, she said, "I have dry clothes in my car."

"I'll go get them. Which bag?"

"The green-striped canvas one on the passenger seat." She reached into her pocket, pulling out her key ring. "It's the big square one."

He loped down the steps and back out into the rain. Miranda tried not to stare at him. But the image of bunching leg muscles and buttocks stayed firmly in her mind. What did his bare legs look like? His chest had a light mat of hair. Would his legs be hairy? What color was the hair? Stop it! she ordered herself.

While she waited, she studied the porch. A battered lawn chair stood guard in one corner and a basket with wood shavings lay in the other. The place was neat and tidy. She wasn't surprised. He looked like a man who avoided clutter.

He returned a minute later with her overnight bag slung over his shoulder. She shivered as the cold, wet wind gusted up onto the scant shelter of his porch. A wave of heat seemed to come alive and stretch out of the open door, reaching around her body. Luke nudged her closer to the doorway, but she hesitated.

Luke reached around her and grabbed a worn, dry poncho from somewhere inside the cabin. "Drape this over yourself while you take off those wet clothes."

She hesitated before reaching for the garment. Her fingers brushed the back of his hand and a shiver coursed through her body. He stepped back.

"Turn around," he said, the drawl in his voice lower and deeper than before.

She hesitated.

"I mean now, darlin'. Get changed." The sharp command bore little resemblance to that soft teasing tone of just moments earlier.

She pivoted away from him and stood rooted to the spot like a hundred-year-old sequoia. There was no mistaking the sound of his zipper opening. She pictured him as he'd been earlier in his bath, chest and back naked. Still she couldn't force her fingers to move. Oh, God, help me.

"I'm not watching you, darlin'. You can get changed." Again the words were smooth as honey dripping over her skin. She sighed, wishing for a tenth of his confidence and ease in this situation.

His soft, drawling voice tiptoed down her spine like a cat burglar in an art museum. She heard him walk inside the house and stood there for a moment longer. The night was cold and damp.

Come on, coward, get changed.

She dropped her wet clothing on the floor by her feet and pulled on the clean underwear and khakis. She bent, digging through her bag before she unearthed the long-sleeved thermal top.

Dropping the poncho to the floor, she pulled her shirt over her head and finger combed her wet hair. She peeked into the cabin and found Luke by the fireplace, adding wood to the fire. He'd changed into a flannel shirt and wheat-colored jeans. The cigar he'd put out earlier was lit and clenched between his teeth. Its fragrance now familiar to her.

Stepping over the threshold, she quietly closed the door behind her. Heat seeped through her clothes and into her skin, warming her completely.

The exposed-beam cabin welcomed her like a pair of worn shoes, knowing the fit and feel of her feet. A large stone fireplace dominated one wall of the cabin. Plate glass windows lined another and a bank of glass doors the final. The effect was one of openness. Miranda imagined that on a clear night the stars would seem to be within arms' reach, almost touchable.

A winding staircase led to an open loft, and though the cabin had a definite masculine feel to it, she'd never felt more at home. Not even in the sophisticated home of her childhood or the trendy little condo she'd spent a large chunk of her savings on. She sighed, moving closer to the fire and the man who knelt by the hearth, patiently feeding kindling to the growing blaze. Her inner voice warned her to stay back from Luke Romero, but something drew her closer to him.

"Can I help?"

Luke felt Miranda's presence behind him before she spoke. Her voice was soft and light, playing over his senses like summer rain over the dry ground. He questioned the wisdom of his decision to bring her back here, but didn't like the answer he received from his raging hormones and lonely soul. He bit down on the end of his cigar.

The woman had more thorns than a briar patch and more contradictions than a television preacher. That didn't stop some foolish part of his soul from wanting to know more about her. To unravel the secrets that she kept hidden behind those big gray eyes.

"Have a seat and warm up." He stood and stared down at her, abruptly realizing that the top of her head barely reached his shoulder. She was so tiny. Any doubts he had about letting her find her own way to her cabin died. "I'll be right back with the stew."

He served up venison stew made from meat that he'd cured himself. Living on the mountain reaffirmed his belief in the man he'd become. He'd come a long way from his wild, roaming youth in the rodeo. A long way from the young man who'd watched his best friend die beneath the stomping hooves of a beast. Part of him still longed to prove to his father that he'd made a success of his life without his father's land, approval or the hand-picked wife.

Now he had to deal with a city woman again. A lady with crystal eyes that gleamed with intelligence and fatigue. A lady who was used to control—she bristled at every order he issued—yet here on his mountain was oddly vulnerable. A lady whose body promised pleasure that would lead to trouble.

Why then did exhilaration make the back of his neck tingle? The same outlaw feeling as when he pushed his Harley to the limit. Wearing no helmet, using no common sense and obeying no rules. Just pure thrill and a fear he'd never admit out loud.

"Enough," he said, not realizing he'd spoken out loud until his voice broke the silence that had fallen.

"What?" Miranda asked. The fire's light played over her brown hair, picking out the red highlights and making her seem more untouchable than ever. An ethereal fairy sent to cast a spell over him and make mischief in his life.

"Nothing," he replied gruffly. He forced himself to concentrate on the matter at hand—finishing dinner and getting her safely out of his cabin. He tossed the remains of the cigar into the fire, unable to enjoy it any longer.

"How long will you be vacationing up here?" he asked, needing to know exactly when she'd be leaving so that he'd be able to hunt in her neighborhood again. He wanted to avoid her while she vacationed on his mountain.

"I'm not on vacation."

Luke felt as if he'd been sucker punched by fate. Damn it all. When was life going to stop throwing these tricky little kinks at him? He should have learned that lesson long ago. "So when are you leaving?"

Her mouth curved down and she looked away from him. He heard her take a shaky breath before she glanced back at him. "I haven't decided. A few months, maybe more."

Luke stood and gathered the dishes, dumping them in the sink. The sooner he got her to her cabin the better. He wasn't going to ask her any more questions, though he was tempted to get to know her better. He grabbed his slicker off the peg near the door. "I'll be right back."

The late April rain had let up a little and a sliver of moon lit the sky, the illumination not enough to brighten even a small distance in front of him. Luke cursed as he walked back into the cabin for a flashlight. He didn't want her staying on his mountain tonight or any other night. He didn't want to have to think of her sleeping in that old, decrepit cabin, a soft city woman in his domain. He didn't want to think of those peachy pink lips, crushed beneath his, because if she stayed, he'd kiss her. The temptation was slowly eroding his defenses much the way Mother Nature had worn away the valley that he gazed at each morning. Slowly, but inevitably.

He scanned the room and found Miranda stretching in front of the fireplace. Her arms held high above her head, her breasts pushing against the cotton of her shirt, her eyes closed, and a smile of sensual delight on her face as the fire's warmth played against her skin. Lust hit him—hard. He clenched his fists.

He had to get her out of here before his control snapped.

Before he forgot that he didn't want a woman in his life. Before he forgot that short-term affairs weren't that fulfilling anymore. Before he forgot that he was a loner because life was safer that way.

"Let's go," he said, his voice sounding gritty and deep to his own ears. It was a wonder he didn't frighten her with it.

Her eyes snapped open. All semblance of relaxation vanished. She tensed under his watchful gaze.

"Is it getting worse outside?"

Her husky voice toyed with his mind, creating images he had no business thinking. Images of him and her on the quilt his grandmother had made for him. Clothed only in the fire's light and a sheen of sweat. Luke closed his eyes and counted to ten. Control, he reminded himself. *Ride the beast, don't let the beast ride you.* His father's advice echoed in his head like the unwanted ringing from a hangover.

Though the old man had died fifteen years ago, Luke had never reconciled with him and felt his father's presence as keenly as he felt the absence of the land he should have inherited. He felt it fitting that his father still tried to control his life from beyond the grave. Fitting because he'd had the chance make peace with his father but chose instead to stay silent. A father should believe in his son *always.*

"Yes, but I'll get you to your cabin."

She nodded, sliding her feet into worn deck shoes. Her feet were long and slender with high arches and a delicate peach tint on her toenails. The color only a shade lighter than her lips.

Get busy, he ordered himself. He grabbed a canvas laundry sack from his days on the road with the rodeo, tossing her wet clothes into it. "Do you need anything else from the car for tonight?"

"Yes," she said, slinging the strap of the overnight bag over her shoulder. "I'll go to the car with you."

He realized she didn't have a raincoat. The next time he saw Edgar Jennings he was going to kick his old, gnarled butt down the mountain. Why couldn't he rent his cabin to someone who knew how to pack for this kind of weather? Someone who didn't show up in the middle of the rainy season in a car without four-wheel drive. Someone who looked like Edgar and was about as friendly as a hungry alligator.

But the poncho leaked and the rain showed no sign of letting up. He shrugged out of his slicker and handed it to her. He had a duster upstairs in a box somewhere.

"Use this. I'll be back in a minute."

He climbed the stairs with a carefully measured stride and paused at the top. She stood in the middle of the room staring up at him from those brilliant crystal eyes. "If you go outside, take the flashlight from under the sink."

Luke refused to acknowledge the small tightening as anything other than anger. He grabbed the duster from the bottom of the old cardboard box and ignored the items that spilled onto the floor. He stalked back down the stairs. Picking up her overnight bag and the laundry sack, he went outside.

Miranda stood by her car with a large bag slung over her shoulder and her grocery bag. "This is all I'll need for now."

The spring rain made the roads impossible even for the Suburban. The mountain was treacherous and malevolent toward the foolish and the stupid. Something Luke had learned the hard way. He took the grocery sack from her.

"Thanks."

"Let's go," he said between clenched teeth. The path between his place and Miranda's was difficult in full daylight, at night it was downright dangerous, but not impassable.

Luke cursed under his breath as a wet tree branch smacked against his shoulder. The rain had slowed but the water hung suspended in the leaves, showering them with a cold blast whenever the wind blew.

He shifted the overnight bag to his left hand where he held the flashlight. He reached back to help Miranda over a fallen log. She glanced at his hand, then at his face before placing her hand in his.

She would be happy to be rid of him. But he couldn't leave her to fend for herself. He'd take care of her, whether she wanted him to or not. The thought of her lost out here haunted him like the memory of past mistakes.

A quarter of an hour later the ramshackle old hunting cabin came into view. The lack of light made the small wood structure look like a fright house at the fair. Luke knew from experience that it didn't look much better during the day. But it was fairly sturdy.

He played the light over the front porch, checking for rodents. He glanced at Miranda wondering if she'd change her mind now. If she'd agree to go back to his place and then let him escort her off the mountain in the morning. He expected to see some sign of disappointment or revulsion.

"At last," she said. "Just dump that bag inside the door."

Luke was sure that the fatigue from the long day must have caught up with her. She'd brought a sack of junk food and had only two bags of possessions with her. She stared at that damned eyesore as though it was…home.

He didn't think the run-down cabin was much of anything, but if his alternative housing was a small convertible he guessed he'd be more excited about the shack in front of him.

"Let me check inside," he said gruffly. He didn't want to like her, but he admired her grit. It was the one city trait he could relate to. He figured it was a kickback to Neanderthal times when humans had been forced to carve a place for themselves in the world—only the trappings had changed and the corporate world demanded as much from its challengers as Mother Nature did.

"That's okay. I'll take care of it. I'm sure you want to be on your way."

"This place has been empty since last June. There could be all kinds of critters inside."

"I'll take my chances," she said firmly.

He gritted his teeth. Luke had the feeling he'd just been dismissed. God save him from bossy women, he thought.

"Fine," he said, but hesitated.

"What are you waiting for?" she asked.

Common sense to kick in, he thought wryly. "You to go inside."

She frowned at him—an intimidating expression that made him want to grin. If he'd learned one thing about Miranda, it was that the woman liked things to be her way. He waited, living on the mountain had taught him patience.

"Very well. Thank you again for your help, Mr. Romero."

"No problem, darlin'."

He waited until she disappeared inside through the front door and he saw her light come on. He walked away knowing that it was the sensible thing to do.

A stubborn woman as a neighbor and raging hormones he'd thought he'd finally mastered. He wanted her and he damned himself for it.

Three

Luke's cabin was deserted when Miranda arrived three days later. She left a basket of chocolate chip cookies on the front porch. She'd scraped all of the black burnt stuff off the bottoms and they looked pretty good. Her mother had been so excited when she'd called to get the recipe from her. She'd baked eight dozen cookies, but had only been able to rescue a few.

Determined to tackle nature and take control of her surroundings, she stepped off his porch and retrieved her fishing gear from the ground. She planned on catching dinner today. The thought of eating another peanut-butter-and-jelly sandwich made her cringe. She'd eaten so much junk food in the past two days that she'd had trouble sleeping. Focusing on the disturbing images of those chocolate brown eyes or that twinkling stud earring hadn't helped.

She picked her way across the meadow. The mountain that seemed so malevolent toward her that first night, now apologized with a beautiful spring day. The air still had a chill to it, but the sun promised warmth. She spread her arms and lifted her head, drinking in the beauty that surrounded her.

The tow-truck driver who had dropped her car off this morning had talked endlessly about the weather, the tourist season and the wildflowers blooming in the meadow. Friendly chitchat that had no point. She'd been at a loss as to what to say. Miranda wanted to ask questions about Luke but knew in a small community such as this one the gossip would flow steadily out of control. So instead she'd held her tongue, leaving her imagination free to create whatever images it wanted to.

The detailed tattoo danced through her mind. The tanned skin underneath the hawk made her fingers long to caress him. She wanted to test the resilience of the padded muscles on his back.

Enough, she thought. Her laptop computer and modem would be installed tomorrow afternoon. She wanted something to occupy her time. The mountain, though pretty, still wasn't an environment she felt comfortable in. Her adjustment time was taking longer than she'd expected, but the only obstacle she'd been unable to conquer was her own body's weakness. She knew in a few weeks she'd find the balance she was seeking and she'd have something familiar to concentrate on instead of Luke Romero and his disturbing sensuality.

She found the stream and spent a few minutes picking through the grass and debris left by the storm until she found the perfect spot.

Clean, clear water rustled softly, winding its way downstream. The fish swimming at the bottom were visible and a crisp fresh scent of wildflowers filled the air. She stood perfectly still for a moment letting nature's beauty soak into the fabric of her being.

"Okay," she muttered to herself.

The *Field and Stream* magazine she'd purchased before

leaving Atlanta had a few pictures of fishermen—all of them standing in the middle of a stream in hip-high waders. She wanted to cast from the relative safety of the bank.

She'd baited the hook easily, having no trouble imagining the squirmy little worm as her ex-fiancé. It was petty and spiteful, but worked darn well.

She glanced at the book on the ground and then back at her rod and reel. It should be easier than this, she thought. Children do this every day.

She stood, mimicking the stance she saw on the magazine's glossy page. She raised her arm over her head and tried to copy the wrist-snapping motion she'd seen others use. She hooked something before she landed the line in the water. She started to reel it in, but the line grew taut and wouldn't budge.

Miranda set the pole on the ground and grimaced at the branch of the tree holding her hook captive. The lowest branches were too high for her grab hold of and swing herself into the tree. She doubted she'd be able to scale the trunk without help. But what kind of help?

She was alone in the forest, miles from civilization and her only neighbor was a man who wanted nothing to do with her. Besides, the role of helpless woman wasn't one she wanted to play. She tugged on the line, hoping to free the hook, but the lure tightened its grip on the small branch and hung on.

Jumping, she latched onto a sturdy branch and tried to wiggle her way up the trunk. Her sweaty hands slid on the bark and she slid back toward the ground. She hung suspended.

"Great," she muttered.

"Need some help?"

Miranda screamed and fell to the ground. She braced herself, ready to do battle. Luke Romero stood there looking...she struggled to describe the expression in his eyes.

He looked as if he didn't want to be at this place at this time.

"Can you free my line?"

He rocked back on his heels, staring up at the large tree. The fishing pole swayed with the branches.

"Maybe." He paced under the branches for a few minutes. "Stand back."

He leapt, catching the lowest branch and then pulled himself up the tree. Miranda watched the graceful movements with envy and awe. Luke moved like a man sure of himself and his environment.

Today, his hair was held off his neck in a ponytail and his Stetson was nowhere to be found. The bill of a faded baseball cap was tucked into the back pocket of illegally tight jeans. A small hoop earring hung through his ear, enforcing his outlaw image, and the pungent scent of a cigar lingered on his clothes. He looked like a pirate who had been at sea for too long.

He freed her line and joined her on the ground. "Here you go."

"Thanks," she said, watching his large hands move carefully over the hook, freeing bits of greenery from its teeth. She wondered if they'd handle a woman with the same attention.

"No problem," he said.

He handed the fishing pole to her, before pulling the baseball cap out of his back pocket and putting it on.

"Thanks for the cookies."

Miranda blushed, wondering if he'd actually eaten one. "Did you try them?"

"Yeah," he said, grinning suddenly. "Well, you know, they weren't the greatest cookies I've ever had." His voice was so soft she had a hard time hearing the next words. "But no one's ever baked anything for me before."

Miranda felt a tiny clenching around her heart and all her maternal instincts urged her to reach out to the boy inside of Luke and comfort him. *Maternal instincts,* she thought with a touch of sadness. Was it possible for a woman who couldn't have kids to be maternal? She'd never thought so until that very moment.

His gaze met hers, his brown eyes full of emotion and pain. She started to touch him, then stopped. Her hand hung awkwardly between them. The tanned shade of his skin made hers look pale.

"It was a first for me, too," she said at last, dropping her hand.

He smiled. Miranda felt something open up inside of her that she'd thought she'd lost. Something rare and fragile that reminded her of childhood and the days of wonder. Something beautiful and scary but she refused to analyze it now.

Miranda's soft laughter echoed the sound of the water tripping over the rocks downstream. The rippling effect spread slowly throughout his body. He'd warned himself to stay away from her. Knew that he shouldn't have left the safety of the north face of the mountain where she would never wander. Knew that he should've gotten on the Harley and gone to town. Knew that this was the worst possible thing for him to be doing, but he stayed all the same.

The sunlight dripped through the leaves of the trees that surrounded the bank, bathing Miranda in its golden light. Her skin had the same hue as orange-blossom honey. Soft, light and tempting as hell. The urge to taste her was overwhelming, to lick at her skin until the essence of her was imbedded in his senses. But he fought it.

He groaned, picking up the fishing pole he'd set aside a half hour earlier. Time to put things in their proper perspective. He'd known he was in trouble when he opened the lid on that basket and seen the cookies lying inside. No one ever made cookies for him.

His mother died long before he was able to chew them on his own and his dad's girlfriends weren't the type to spend time in the kitchen. The cookies were definitely the worst he'd ever tasted but that didn't matter. It was the thought that counted.

"Ready to catch your supper?"

She nodded. "I'm guessing you don't need the magazine to show you how to stand."

"What magazine?"

She lifted a new issue of *Field and Stream,* showing him the marked page. "It's just as well, these instructions got me into trouble the first time."

"Darlin', that man is fly-fishing." The picture reminded him of years earlier when he and his estranged brother Jake had spent a weekend at the river. Luke scowled and pushed the memory aside, ignoring the remembered camaraderie. Jake's betrayal was all he wanted to associate with his brother.

"I know. I figured I'd better use this pole. Fly-fishing looks very complicated."

"It is. But you have to use a different stroke with this pole."

She flushed. It had been a long time since he'd seen a woman color at a suggestive remark. He pretended that her reaction didn't warm his heart.

"What kind of stroke?" she asked, her voice husky with suppressed emotion.

"A delicate stroke, one that builds anticipation. A teasing stroke that makes the fish think you've been there all along. A tempting stroke that'll lead her right into your trap."

"Stop it," she said.

He showed her how to fish, leaving off the words he'd been using to entice her. He demonstrated the casting technique before handing the rod to Miranda. She reeled in her first catch of weeds a few seconds later. The lady simply didn't have the right swing.

Luke stepped behind her. Her floral perfume wrapped around his senses like a warm breeze on a cool day. He cursed himself as a fool but reached around and took the fishing pole from her hands. She started as his chest brushed against her back. The soft, rounded curves of her hips were a temptation he couldn't ignore. The urge to drop the fishing pole and sink his fingers into her flesh almost overpowered him. Instead, he forced himself to strip the weeds from the hook.

"Do you really want to learn how to fish?" he asked, hoping for a negative answer. Yet, at the same time he knew he didn't have to stay. That the only reason he was still here was because she'd given him those rotten-tasting cookies. A sweet gesture from a prickly woman.

"Yes."

Damn, he cursed silently, then took a deep breath. Inhaling more than air, inhaling the very essence of the tiny woman standing next to him. So close, but farther away than Miami at the moment. "I'm going to put my hands over yours and show you how to cast."

"Okay," she said, turning to face him with her hands extended.

Great idea, he thought. Perfect way to avoid his raging hormones and her sweet curves, but it wouldn't work.

"Turn around, darlin'. You've got to face the stream to catch fish."

She followed his directions, standing stiffly in front of him. "What now?"

He walked closer to her, allowing only an inch of space between them. "I'm going to put my arms around you. Place your hands on the pole so that you can feel the flow of the cast."

He demonstrated the overhead motion of his arm, releasing the line slowly as it came over their heads. The lure landed in the middle of the stream without so much as a ripple.

"Now, comes the tricky part," he whispered, directly into her ear. "Waiting. Stay perfectly still."

A lone trout swam close to the lure. "Watch carefully. This is where luck doesn't count. It's just you and the fish and you have to be patient...until... Come on, baby. That's it, take the bait, you know you want it."

Luke continued talking in that low modulated tone. The way his daddy had taught him to, years before when he was more a boy than a man. Back when his father had still respected him. Miranda relaxed against him, letting his body direct hers. Her hands still held ready over his and then slowly the speckled fish took the bait. He felt her backbone stiffen with excitement.

"Don't lose it now with impatience. Let him get a good hold on the worm and pull it in slowly. *Now.*"

Luke reeled in the fish. Miranda ducked under his arms and grabbed a net to put the trout in. He unhooked the fish and placed him in the net Miranda held.

"Now what?" she asked.

"Did you bring a cooler?"

"I thought that was only used to hold beer, so I left it at home." Her brow wrinkled as she searched her meager supplies for something to put the fish in. "Fishing is more complicated than I was led to believe."

Luke couldn't help himself. She sounded so disgruntled and looked so cute with her navy shorts and baggy T-shirt that he hugged her to his side in a quick embrace. "Don't worry, darlin'. This guy's too small to keep."

"Great," she muttered.

Luke tossed the fish back into the stream with a powerful motion of his wrist. The trout hit the water and swam quickly away. "Why don't you practice while I go back for a cooler?"

"Okay," she said, her gaze fixed on the worm bucket.

"Want me to bait the hook before I go?"

She gave him a look so haughty it made him want to kiss her. She had so many contradictions.

"I like this part," she said. A huge grin spread across her face like dawn creeping past the power of the night.

"Why?" he asked, unable to fathom what she'd find amusing about baiting the hook.

She blushed but refused to answer. Luke turned away without pushing. He'd broken some major rules today but somehow that didn't seem to matter. A part of his soul felt lighter—almost as if it'd come home. He hadn't realized that home could be a feeling and not a place. He'd thought of his home as always being lost to him, the ranch house and acreage in West Texas gone forever. He didn't want to question why, but knew the answer was sitting beside a cool mountain stream, fishing.

Miranda watched the last rays of the setting sun dip beneath the horizon. She'd been back from her fishing expedition for a few hours. She washed her hands under the outdoor spigot and glanced at her watch. She had less than ten minutes to get over to Luke's place. Her hands shook as she dried them with the towel.

Hurrying inside, she changed into a pair of baggy khaki shorts and a short-sleeved oxford-style shirt. Standing in front of the mirror she wished she were anyone else. She wanted to be more like the women she'd seen who'd been at ease with men, but her career had always been first. She'd been sixteen when her doctor had told her she'd never be able to have kids. She'd overheard her father saying that marriage would never be an option for her. Miranda had focused on her education and career, following her dad into finance. Until Warren came along, pursuing her and saying he wanted a marriage without kids, allowing her to keep her secret. She didn't really know how to entice a man and in her heart she knew disappointment would follow if she did succeed in seducing the sexy mountain man who lived so close to her.

She'd invited Luke on impulse. He'd accepted, but only after insisting that he cook their dinner at his place. She went down the hall to the kitchen where she cut up the vegetables for the salad. She sealed the salad in a plastic container and added it to the cooler where she'd placed a bottle of wine.

Single living was lonely on the side of the mountain. Maybe that was why she kept finding excuses to visit her neighbor. She didn't even know who owned the town house next to hers in Atlanta. She had three friends and they were all through work. She'd never gone out of her way to encourage anyone to be close to her, preferring her own company.

But she wanted someone else's company now. Not just anyone's, she admitted to herself—Luke Romero's.

She paused at the edge of his property. He was singing again. One of those sad love songs that made her heart weep. She almost turned back, afraid to confront him lest he was bathing again, but then he stopped singing.

She crept around the side of the house, finding an empty tub. Whispering a silent prayer of thanks, she glanced around for Luke. He faced the empty meadow that was his backyard, his head bent and hands on his hips.

The utterly masculine pose took her breath away. A black T-shirt molded to the thick muscles of his back and tight jeans conformed to his legs. He was all man—more man than she'd ever encountered.

He raised his hands to his mouth and the sound of a blues harmonica filled the air. The music drew her closer to him. She couldn't turn away from that slow, sensuous sound if her life depended on it.

Her blood started pulsing in beat with the music. A strange sort of lethargy stole through her bones. She wanted to be closer to the source of the sound. Setting the cooler on the steps of the back porch, she approached Luke.

He continued to play but turned toward her. His deep brown eyes watched her like a trapped wolf waiting for the death knell. She knew that this was a side he didn't like people to see. Something precious and rare unfolded inside her. She had one chance to grab hold of this emotion before it disappeared forever. One chance to experience a *real* man and *real* passion.

She took another step toward him.

He stopped playing. The hand holding the harmonica dropped to his side. He stared at her as if he'd never seen her kind before; as if she were the first woman to invade his world; as if she were the only woman he was hungry for. The only woman he needed or wanted in his life, but Miranda knew that it was only an illusion and she was seeing what she wanted to see, not what was really there. *No man could ever really want her.*

Long moments of silence fell between them and the creatures of the night began their daily symphony filling the meadow with sounds so sweet that only Luke's harmonica could compete with them. Miranda wrapped her arms around her waist, trying desperately to remember why she'd come here.

But before she remembered, Luke paced to her—stopping only when his breath brushed her face. He smelled of mint, cigar and coffee. She opened her mouth, breathing in his breath, tasting something more than the caffeine, the tobacco and the freshness; tasting something so essentially male that it unnerved her.

"I brought a salad and wine," she said into the silence.

He nodded but didn't say a word. Only continued to stand there, towering above her like a pagan god of ancient times. She cleared her throat and took a step back, putting distance between herself and this man before something happened. Something that she wouldn't be able to control.

"What took you so long?" he asked, his hot gaze running over her, leaving a slow burning in its wake.

What had he said? He stared at her lips and they tingled. She ached to know the taste and feel of his mouth. Would it be as fulfilling as the teasing breath had promised?

"I'm three minutes early," she said, unable to keep quiet. "I brought a book that demonstrates how to grill trout on an open fire."

"I've grilled before so you can hold on to that book." Amusement was clear in his voice. She remembered the *Field and Stream* magazine fiasco and shook her head.

Miranda didn't know why she felt like a teenager all over again. But something about Luke brought to mind those long, lonely days when she'd felt excited, nervous and unsure of the future. She forgot the sophistication she'd carefully cultivated in the intervening years. *Damn.*

He smiled. His teeth white against the rough, tanned skin of his face. He had a nice mouth, with lips that tempted her to lean closer, to taste him. To trace the individual serrations of his teeth with her tongue. To feel it moving over her own with the same precision he'd used to play the harmonica.

She felt the honey of his drawl before the words left his mouth. "Since you went to all the trouble of making the salad and bringing the wine, I'll clean the fish."

"I was hoping you'd say that."

He chuckled and the sound of his laughter filled the meadow as his music had earlier. Miranda couldn't help the giddy feeling that washed over her. Luke joined hands with her. The feel of his palm brushing against her own was strangely disquieting.

She shivered as something indefinable moved between them. A current that was both shocking and alive pulsed through her veins. A feeling she should ignore, but never could because it was so strange and new. A type of passion she thought she'd never experience.

Luke brought their joined hands to his lips. His mouth brushing lightly over her fingers. A shiver of anticipation ran through her, making her tremble visibly.

"What's the matter, darlin'?"

She shook her head, unable to speak.

"Afraid I'll demand something in return for fixing dinner?" The bitterness in his tone surprised her, following on the heels of his laughter.

"No," she said, hardly recognizing the husky voice as her own. "Afraid you won't."

Four

Afraid you won't.

The words echoed in her head as she followed Luke into the house. What had she been thinking? She hadn't been. For the first time in her life she'd lived for the moment and it backfired. Dead silence had followed her bold response before Luke turned aside her words. Smoothing over her own embarrassment at behaving so forwardly, she allowed him to lead her into the house for dinner. Maybe the emotions she'd been preparing to reveal had been too much for their short acquaintance.

Miranda sat on a bar stool at the kitchen counter and watched Luke move. She appreciated Luke's effort, her one attempt in the kitchen demonstrated how hard that talent could be.

He had a kind of graceful male beauty she'd never encountered before. His long hair and cowboy boots were out of step with what she'd come to expect. He'd be at home on a ranch in Texas or Wyoming, sharing the joking and camaraderie that went along with Western life. But instead he lived in isolation on top of this mountain.

But he hadn't taken her up on her offer of a kiss and maybe more. Many men would have, yet beneath that rugged veneer, Luke Romero was a good man. Maybe too good for a woman who wasn't whole.

He set his Stetson on the counter to begin dinner preparations. The cowboy hat reminded her that she wanted to ask him about his lack of a horse.

He handed her a glass of wine poured from the bottle she'd brought. An expensive label her friend Lynn had given her the day she'd handed in her resignation. Lynn would approve of her sharing it with Luke now. Her friend was forever trying to fix her up with single guys in the city in hopes that one of those sophisticated men could bring her out of her shell. Thinking of those dates now, she knew why she'd never felt an inkling of interest.

Luke hardly resembled the cool, cultured men she usually encountered in Atlanta. The roughness in his character drew her to him the way a short-term, high-yield, no-risk stock drew brokers from across the country. She reveled in it.

"Did you grow up out West?" she asked abruptly. She'd lost her social polish and panache when it came to this man. A serious conversation would reveal her own interest in him and she had no idea how to control or conceal her emotions. A fever unlike any she'd ever known swept through her. She knew it was desire, but never expected to experience it.

"Yeah, darlin', I did. On a ranch in West Texas. Nothing out there but horses, cattle and endless sky."

The words brought to mind old Clint Eastwood cowboy movies. His voice had a poignant quality, the same one her grandmother used when talking about the Old Country of her youth. The bittersweet time before war had torn Germany apart and destroyed Nana's family.

"Where's your horse?" she asked, needing to delve into every personal secret this man had. Needing to know everything about him so her obsession with him would end.

He gutted the fish with a smooth motion of a lethally sharp knife, his concentration solely on the job at hand. Miranda wondered if he'd heard her question. Perhaps she was edging into forbidden territory with her questions. The silence built around them.

He cleared his throat before taking a sip of his wine. The stemmed glass seemed fragile nestled in his large hand. The aura of power that surrounded him reminded her of the first night they'd met. He'd handled every obstacle the mountain and nature had thrown at them. He fit effortlessly into this environment.

"How do you know I've got one?"

She fiddled nervously with her wineglass. "You look like you should."

"Why?"

She couldn't tell if he was teasing or if he really wanted to know. It was the way he walked—a masculine stride that imbued each step with an unconscious sexiness, but with a slight bowleggedness that made her think he must have spent significant time on a horse at some point in his life.

She shrugged, not sure what answer to give.

"I used to," he said. He arched one eyebrow at her in a way she found totally sexy.

She could hardly break contact with those deep brown eyes. God, he stirred something inside her that she didn't know how to control.

"What happened?" she asked, needing to know more.

"About fifteen years ago my father and I had a disagreement. I left the ranch and haven't been home since."

"Is that all?" She'd fought with her parents numerous times.

He stared at her as if trying to ascertain if her interest was genuine or merely curiosity.

"My father said he wished he'd never see me again, and I was happy to oblige him."

The words, simple and succinct, hid emotions she couldn't begin to fathom. True, her relationship with her father wasn't a good one, but she still knew she could go home if she wanted to. Parents always expected you to be so much more than human, Miranda thought.

"Is it ever possible to live up to a parent's expectations?" she asked softly.

"I doubt it. But he would've approved of my riding in the rodeo after I left the ranch."

"Tell me about the rodeo. Did you ride horses there?"

He finished filleting the trout, but accepted the change in topics without comment. "Well, darlin', I'm one of those crazy guys who couldn't figure out why we didn't ride the cows."

Miranda knew that he was telling her something important about himself. Something that she should pay attention to because of the pain in his eyes. She leaned forward wanting to touch him and soothe the pain she felt emanating from him, but knowing she had no right. Clenching her hands into fists, she stifled the urge.

"Why'd you want to ride the cows?" she asked, not sure that she understood what he was talking about. "I thought ranchers milked or butchered livestock."

"Not cows, darlin'," he said, his voice taking on a dark tone. "I meant bulls. I forgot you're not familiar with rodeo lingo."

Bulls. That one word confirmed what she'd already knew in her heart. The man who could make her soul weep while he played the harmonica was an outlaw. One of those men who constantly challenged life. Someone who didn't have to buy a thrill or live vicariously on the stock market.

"Isn't that dangerous?" she asked.

"Yeah, it is. Many a friend has been maimed riding the circuit."

She felt shaky and weak at the thought of Luke getting hurt. Unable to mask the huskiness in her voice, she asked, "When do you ride again?"

"I don't. I stopped riding rodeo a few years ago. The rodeo is a game for the young. It can make a man old before his time. If he's lucky."

Thank God. The relief that coursed through her made her shudder.

"And if he's not lucky?"

"Then he doesn't get to retire."

He was talking about death. She shuddered. The most danger she'd ever faced was a white sale at Sak's on a Saturday morning.

"You live a quiet life now?" she asked, with more interest than was safe.

"Quiet meaning dull?"

She nodded.

"Hell, no, darlin'. Life's no fun that way."

Miranda watched the man who was so far removed from her way of life that he could have been from another planet. He prepared their dinner and they talked about books they'd read, current events and the weather. But nothing personal, and that disappointed her.

Luke directed Miranda outside after dinner and watched as she sat down in his favorite redwood chair. The possessiveness he felt at seeing her in his home hadn't disappeared, but neither had his self-control. He lit a cigar and took a deep drag.

The softening in her eyes and the concern evident in her voice earlier announced she cared for him. No one had ever really cared for him before. Well, he'd thought he'd had it once with his wife and son, but he'd been easily replaced. Not even when he'd spent long, endless summer days pitting himself against one of nature's fiercer beasts. And while he would like nothing more than to indulge in a summer affair with her, he needed more. His last fling had ended badly and though he wanted Miranda like hell's inhabitants wanted ice water, he wouldn't take her. He couldn't take her because he valued the friendship that he was beginning to have with this polished professional.

"What made you leave the city?" he asked, leaning against the railing. Her shorts ended at the knees, the smooth length of her calf had been teasing him all evening. He wanted to reach out and caress her.

"How do you know I'm from the city?" She evaded his question playfully. The two glasses of wine she'd consumed with dinner loosening her innate resolve. She fiddled with the steam of the wineglass and stared up at the stars.

"I meant you look like money. You're dressed for an evening on the town, not a night in the woods. Your clothing, conversation and even the wine are all *big city*, the *right* address."

She blushed at the words. "Well, you're certainly no country bumpkin yourself, Romero. Those boots don't come cheap."

He glanced down at the battered Tony Lamas on his feet. They were expensive—old, but expensive. There was a difference between having money and being from the city.

"There's no way you'll ever convince me you were raised on a ranch."

"I wasn't. Just because I grew up in the city doesn't mean I'm used to money. I worked hard for everything I have, and if I want to wear Italian leather uppers to walk through the woods, I will."

"Whoa, there, darlin'. I didn't mean anything by those comments. I really wanted to know why you're up here."

He sensed her reluctance to discuss her past. The night sounds grew louder as she retreated into her own thoughts. Miranda started when a bullfrog croaked. "You don't have to tell me," he said.

"I'm an executive at Baily, Dillion, and Partners. It's an investment firm."

"Are you on leave?"

"No, at least I don't think so. I tried to resign but my boss is considering this a personal leave."

"What are you going to do?" he asked, needing to understand the conflicting emotions in her voice.

"Nothing. Mark isn't expecting an answer until August. It's our fiscal year-end."

He had the ridiculous urge to enfold her in a bear hug. She sounded lost. As if she didn't have anything left to achieve. As if she'd worked hard for one goal and then upon reaching it, found that it wasn't worth the long hours.

He thought he might be able to give her something else to concentrate on. His lips and body. He longed to taste her. It was all he'd been able to think about since she'd arrived.

Miranda just wasn't a city girl, she was a top-notch businesswoman. No matter how much she liked the fresh air and outdoors, someday she'd go back to the five-star restaurants and exclusive shopping boutiques of her big city. He didn't even know which one she came from.

New York, Los Angeles or Atlanta, it didn't really matter. The distance between their two life-styles was as big as the Pacific Ocean. He'd never be able to bridge it. He wasn't even sure he wanted to.

He stood over her, clenching his fists to keep from touching her. She studied her hands. "You look too young to be an executive."

"I'm not as young as you think I am," she said wryly.

He hesitated, knowing women didn't like to reveal their ages. "Well, I'm thirty-six, so you look young to me. What are you twenty-four, twenty-five?"

"*Twenty-eight.* I started college early."

He hadn't gone at all. Sure he read the newspaper and kept up with current events, but he always regretted the lack of a formal education. Miranda hadn't sounded condescending, but a lot of women talked down to him as if his lack of schooling—namely a degree—meant he couldn't comprehend *any* complex business issues or events.

Instead of dwelling on his shortcomings, he wondered how much of life she'd missed by going straight to college.

"Bet you learned how to slow dance at frat parties."

She shook her head. "Never went to one party. I pushed through school in two years."

The short length of her hair was ruffled by a slight breeze. She didn't look like a corporate executive, instead she seemed like his own personal fairy sent to enchant and bemuse him before wreaking havoc with his life. He set his cigar on the railing. Finally he had the excuse he needed to touch her. Just hold her, he promised himself. A light brushing of bodies nothing more.

"Want to learn?"

By way of answering, she stood and set her glass on the deck. He swept her into his arms. *At last.* The sounds of nature filled the meadow, providing music. Their footsteps as they two-stepped around the porch provided a rhythmic counterpoint. He felt the jungle beating of his blood all the way to his soul and wanted to pull her closer.

The warm woman in his arms felt right. Somehow he'd forgotten what it was like to hold a woman in his arms and tease himself with the beginning stages of arousal. His body stirred as the slight floral scent she wore wafted up toward him. She smelled like spring and he felt like frozen winter. *Thaw me,* he thought. She snuggled closer and her words of earlier this evening came back to him.

Afraid you won't.

Suddenly he felt like demanding something from her. Something hot, deep and physical. Something more than a kiss but less than actual fulfillment. Something he needed…

"We need music," he said, his voice a deeper, huskier version. He thrust away from her, heading for the house.

He'd bring the boom box out and play some rowdy Cajun music. That would keep his thoughts off her body.

"Luke?"

He stopped. She stood bathed in the faint light spilling from the house and the moonbeams trickling though the cloudy night. She looked like a woman on the cusp of change. She looked like a woman who could fulfill a man's every fantasy.

Miranda crossed to him, her hand on his forearm. "Will you sing?"

"When'd you hear me sing?"

"I watched you in your bath the day we met."

A blush suffused her face. A wave of dark red covered her neck, cheeks and forehead all the way to her hairline. He'd never seen anyone color the way she had. She refused to glance above his collar. She cleared her throat.

Her voice sounded deeper, huskier than usual. She still refused to meet his gaze, but he lifted her chin. Her gray eyes were foggy, concealing what she really felt.

"I'm guessing you're not talking about that little ditty about the woman in the bar."

"No," she said softly. She rested her head on his breastbone—right over his heart. *Damn.* He tried to ignore the contentment spreading throughout his body. The woman had wormed her way past his defenses without even trying.

He began to sing, his voice low-pitched. She hummed a counter melody. Luke told himself it didn't matter if their voices blended as easily as their bodies would. It didn't matter if her curves fit into his hollows as if she were made to be his. It didn't matter if she felt right in his arms.

He knew she didn't belong there.

He stopped singing abruptly and pushed away from her. She tightened her grip on his neck. Her breath brushed his neck as she sighed.

"Don't," he said, trying to let her know that he had to let go. But it was too late. He wanted—no *needed*—to kiss her. Needed to know if she'd taste as good as he knew she would. If she'd respond with the same passion and enthusiasm she'd shown for fishing and eating. If she'd react like dynamite—going up in his arms and setting fire to his body and soul.

Luke bent and tasted the pink lips that had haunted his dreams for days, making sleep a distant memory. She yielded to him as if she'd been hungry for the same thing. An uncontrollable wildness pulsed through his veins.

He rubbed the back of her neck, sweeping his hands down to the firm curve of her hips. Sinking his fingers into the resilient flesh as he'd dreamed of doing earlier. Her waist was so tiny he could span it with his hands. The bounty of her body bloomed both above and below.

He kissed her as if she were the only woman on earth. Her taste became imbedded in his senses. Somewhere deep inside he felt a tearing, a complete ripping of the last un-jaded part of his soul.

Miranda's lips opened under the pressure of his. Luke felt as if someone had touched a live wire to his soul. The battered, scarred part of his psyche was jolted back to life by her presence. Her taste was sweeter than he'd imagined any woman's could be. Her mouth was hotter and more potent than his first illegal sip of whiskey. He'd never felt anything half as right in all his days.

Luke refused to think about the consequences. He wanted to revel in the emotions she drew forth from the center of his soul. Revel in the feelings he'd thought he'd banished completely. Revel in this woman who was slowly reminding him what it meant to be alive.

Luke cradled her closer. The soft sounds she made in the back of her throat inflamed him, eating away at his self-control. Would she make the same sounds as he thrust into her warm body? Would she welcome him the same way she welcomed him now? Or was this one of those games women liked to play?

She moved against him with surprising strength, her passion running as hot as his. He'd never had a woman react so quickly to his sensual lure. Never experienced a tenth of the desire he now felt for her—for Miranda. Never experienced a complete lack of control. If he didn't stop this now, he never would.

He lifted his head, breaking contact with her mouth, but still touched her cheeks with his fingers. Her skin was softer than the sheepskin rug on his living room floor. Her scent more enticing than the flower blossoms in spring. Her touch more intoxicating than a bottle of hundred-proof moonshine.

He rubbed his hand down the fragile length of her spine. Her breathing slowly returned to normal and he felt the edges of control wrapping back around him.

His body still clamored for him to carry her inside and strip her naked. To bury his aching flesh inside her petite body and make her his. It was an ancient, primitive feeling over which he had no control.

"Luke?"

He set her away from him, pacing to the railing to stare out at the night sky, the open meadow, anything but the sweet, tempting woman staring at him with crystal gray eyes. Eyes that burned with the fire of desire and the need to know more of his embrace.

"Yeah, darlin'?"

"I didn't come to the mountains to have an affair. A summer fling has never appealed to me."

"Ah, hell, woman. I know that."

He heard her footsteps as she crossed the porch and began to leave. "It's just that you almost made me forget my rules."

Five

"**W**ait."

Luke's husky voice grated across her aroused senses like a cool wind across bare skin, bringing her excited flesh to attention. Actually, she'd been almost running. She needed to escape the pain, the humiliation, the passion he'd brought forth so easily.

She started to turn to face him and realized that her nipples had hardened against her lacy bra. Would he be able to see her reaction to him? She drew in a quivering breath and stopped.

She wanted him.

For the first time in her life Miranda Colby lusted after a man. Not just any man, but Luke Romero with his sad haunting music, rough-edged charm and penchant for exuberant living. She wanted to feel his hard body over hers, rubbing over her breasts which tingled. She wanted his weight settling firmly between her legs and his mouth back on hers. *And that was only the beginning.*

"Turn around," he said, his voice still husky, but more controlled than it had been only a moment earlier.

"No," she said, unsure of her emotions for the first time in her entire adult life. Even hearing Warren break their engagement hadn't had this effect on her. She was shaky and her stomach ached. She had a moment's fear of being physically ill.

She was unsure of a man for the first time in her life. Always in the past it had been easy to pigeonhole a man, to put him in one place in her life, work or...work. But with Luke, she felt much the same as she had on her first day in the vice president's office. Never had a man inspired this feeling.

She heard his footsteps behind her and stiffened. Part of her wanted to hear an explanation for the intense embrace and shatteringly abrupt ending, but the cowardly part of her soul longed for escape. Luke had made her problems seem small, inconsequential and her desire for him a monumental thing. She needed to find safety and comfort in her surroundings and rebuild her inner walls. *As if she'd ever be the same again.*

His hands settled on her shoulders in an unbreakable grip. Her senses began to pulse in time with her heartbeat. The heat of his body engulfed hers. She swayed, brushing against his hard chest. She wished she'd slid her hands under his T-shirt while he'd been kissing her so that she could know those muscles by feel.

She wanted to stay in his embrace, to pull his arms around her and wrap herself in his warmth. But reality was a different matter. She was inexperienced and unable to have kids. If any two things combined could make a woman undesirable to men, it was those two traits.

She was scared.

Warren, her ex-fiancé, had liked her in the beginning and thought she'd make him a good wife and life partner. Both of them had been dedicated to their careers and getting ahead, but after a visit with his family over Easter, he'd started to want a family—the one thing she couldn't provide and had hoped to hide. He suggested she quit so that she'd have time for their children. She'd never forget the feeling of complete helplessness that she'd felt when she'd told him she couldn't have kids but would look into adoption.

Luke frightened her because she wanted him physically with an intensity she'd never experienced before. Warren had wanted to wait until they were married to consummate their relationship once he'd found out she hadn't been with a man. After he'd broken their engagement, she'd been glad that they'd waited.

Luke's ragged breathing filled the air and Miranda's confusion grew. Did he want her—Miranda Colby? Or any woman? Though escape was the one thing she craved, she wasn't leaving him until she found the answer.

She pivoted to face him. The tension she read in his face confused her. Did he regret kissing her? Why had he stopped her from leaving? "Why did you kiss me?"

The moonlight shone down on him, casting his face more in shadow than in light. "Because I had to."

"Why?" she asked, because she'd never had a man kiss her like that before.

"I want you like hell on fire, darlin', and that's just the beginning. I can barely control this…this need for you. But I'm damned if I'm going to let my hormones rule my actions."

She had no response to that. No way of expressing how those blunt words affected her. Never had she driven a man past the limits of his own control. She could hardly believe she'd done so now.

Luke was a man of contradictions, of integrity and honor. The way he'd rushed out in the rain the night they met to help her with her car proved her point. He was a man who was considerate of others. A man who seemed as unsettled by their embrace as she was. Or maybe he was just being nice. That explained it, she thought. Disappointment laced with relief lanced through her.

"Oh, Luke, you're a very kind man."

He laughed a harsh brittle sound that bore no resemblance to the usual sound of his laughter. "I'm not a kind man."

"Yes, you are." Any man who senses a woman's insecurities and tries to reassure her is a kind man.

"Why do you think I'm kind?"

She doubted he'd ever truly understand what she meant, half doubting that she understood it herself. He'd given her something so precious in those moments of passion. Something almost magical because she'd forgotten what she was.

"I meant it in a different way," she said. Feeling brave, she leaned up and brushed her lips across his. She wanted to repay him for the gift he'd unwittingly given her.

"Darlin', I knew you were trouble the first time I laid eyes on you."

The tone of those words didn't make that sound like a bad thing. Knowing they were on the verge of goodbye, she longed to delay her departure, but knew that wasn't wise. The way she felt right now she might start crying at seeing the one thing she really wanted and not having it.

"I'll walk you home."

His gravelly voice reminded her of the song he'd sung earlier. She sighed, a deep sound of contentment that she barely recognized as her own.

"No, thanks. I'd better go alone."

"The woods are dangerous."

"If I can survive in the concrete jungle, I can manage in the woods."

But the concrete jungle had betrayed her, she thought abruptly. The intensity of the emotions she'd experienced tonight convinced her she couldn't get involved with Luke. She wouldn't survive a betrayal from him. She'd stay on her side of the mountain until August and he'd stay on his. He wouldn't follow her and offer to teach her any other outdoor skills. She was going to have to make some serious career decisions before summer's end and she didn't want to let an affair with Luke influence her.

If she allowed herself to be in his company, to get to know the man behind the Stetson, the hawk and the earring, she'd fall in love with him. Already the seeds of caring were taking root in her heart. She couldn't see him again, couldn't kiss him again, couldn't be in his company because to do so would weaken her resolve. She might be tempted to try for the brass ring that was marriage and family, and she knew that it would always remain out of reach for her.

The teakwood dining table he'd been commissioned to carve for a wealthy rancher in Montana served as a catharsis for the unruly emotions trampling through Luke's system. Unreleased desire made his blood simmer and every other thought he had involved Miranda in a provocative pose on that old quilt his grandmother had made for him when he'd left home.

He tried to put her into her place, to make her fit into the role of the women he sometimes got involved with for the summer. Of course, in the past few years, he'd found the pleasure not worth the trouble of driving down the mountain.

He questioned goals and desires that he'd never put into words before. As a young man he'd always yielded to his every impulse, taking all the sweet promise life offered. That overindulgence had caused more pain than the pleasure they had brought. Luke thought he'd gotten past the point where anything could break his will. Thought he'd matured to a man of conviction and honor. But he knew that with Miranda, the need—the *compulsion*—to be with her, could erode defenses that had taken years to get into place.

He wanted her in his bed. For all her sophistication, there was a certain innocence to her. She was unspoiled by the many relationships that women of the nineties often took refuge in. She'd dedicated her life to her career. She'd as much as admitted that she'd never really lived life. Had she ever had an affair?

She didn't have the years of experience that he did. The thought of all those women—nameless, faceless women—sickened him. He'd become so jaded, so cynical toward life in general that he'd retreated to the Smoky Mountains. That and the fact that he'd hated working inside and punching a clock.

He set his knife down and grabbed his Stetson, needing to escape. The confines of his studio made her image seem like a living thing. He felt her presence in his house as surely as she'd been there last night. No other woman had ever dined in his cabin. He wanted to take the Harley and ride down the winding mountain road, but he'd started to work on the engine and wasn't finished.

Despite the fierce hunger in his body for Miranda, he didn't trust her. She'd made herself clear. She was leaving at summer's end. She wanted more than a mountain man could give her. She needed more than satisfaction every night.

He wasn't the man to give it to her.

He would never forget the look of pain on his father's face when Suzanne and *her* son had left. Some things were meant to be lessons, Luke reminded himself. He would never forget the emptiness in his own life after his son was gone. *Only a fool makes the same mistake twice.*

He cursed and grabbed his hunting rifle and extra shells. He needed to hunt before the next rainstorm struck. He was out of meat and couldn't fill his freezer with trout because, ridiculously, fish reminded him of Miranda.

He headed for the face of the mountain where the rough terrain discouraged novice hikers. He wished he'd run into the redneck, good old boys who always trespassed onto his property to poach animals. He needed to release the rowdy blood coursing through his veins and a fistfight was the safest remedy.

He passed through an open meadow where wildflowers bloomed. A small brook meandered through the middle of the field. The sky seemed close enough to touch.

He held his head back, squinting at the sun and letting the wind brush over him. Nature was in a friendly mood today. Not at all the rowdy, stormy side that he loved and enjoyed, but a calm peaceable day that he could appreciate.

A plaid blanket and wicker picnic basket indicated human presence. Luke knew with gut-wrenching surety the alfresco lunch set up belonged to only one person. *Miranda Colby.*

He'd warn her that dangerous men preyed in this area of the mountain. Warned her that she needed to stick to what she knew. Warned her that although she thought him to be a kind man, he wasn't.

What the hell are you doing, boy? Women are good for only one thing—trouble.

He heard his old man's voice as though he was standing next to him watching, waiting for him to screw up again. It wasn't that he doubted that his father was right. The old man had known him too well to be wrong about that. Luke had just finished lecturing himself on the downfalls of getting involved with this woman when he spotted her a few feet into the forest and stopped.

All his words of warning fled. She bathed in the clear, freshwater of the stream. A modest one-piece bathing suit covered her body, but left little to his imagination.

Like a moth drawn to the lethal beauty of an open flame, he stood there staring at her. His loins tightened and his skin felt too small for his bones. His heart beat strongly and he fought the urge to go to her, toss her over his shoulder and carry her back to that plaid blanket.

Hell, he didn't know if he'd make it that far. He wanted her so fiercely he'd take her standing up. The intensity of his desire scared him. Before he could move, she did. She faced the bank and met his gaze squarely.

Her mouth opened on a gasp and he knew she could read the desire in his gaze. Knew she had to be able to see how much he wanted her and how close he was to losing his control. She crossed her arms protectively over her chest.

The cold had tightened her nipples, bringing them to prominence against the wet Lycra suit. Luke's first instinct was to lunge forward, but he didn't.

"Voyeurism?" she asked lightly.

Her attempt at humor failed a bit when it was delivered in a shaking voice. She stepped from the brook, walking gingerly across the rocks and grass.

"You did watch me bathe once," he said, because he really wanted to reach out and grab her. To pull that slim suit off of her and see if her nipples were pink or peachy brown. If they'd bud as tightly for his mouth as they did in reaction to the cold. If they'd taste as hot and sexy as they looked. *Oh, hell.*

"Well, we're even now."

"Not quite, darlin'. I was naked."

"I know," she said. "I've never watched a man bathe before. Don't you have a shower or tub inside?"

"I do. But sometimes the wildness of a storm tempts me outside."

"Was it only the storm that tempted you the night we met?"

"Don't tease me, Miranda, because I want nothing more than to carry you back to the blanket and strip that scrap of clothing off your body. And I won't stop until I'm buried hilt deep in you. Your curves fitting perfectly under my hands and providing a soft counterpoint to my hardness. Is that what you want?"

She looked shaken. Hell, he felt shaken. He was no good at this sort of thing. Picking a woman up for the night was one thing. He could handle that. He even had a certain finesse about him in those situations. But wanting a woman and knowing that he couldn't have her...

"I...I've never had an affair before," she said, her tone light but her gray eyes were filled with confusion, desire and some emotion that Luke didn't know how to define. Was she saying she'd never slept with any man? Surely a woman of her age and sophistication wasn't a virgin.

For once, he was glad of his past. That Suzanne had taught him all there was to know about manipulation, otherwise he'd be tempted to believe the trembling voice of this woman standing before him. He'd be tempted to believe that someday she'd stay with him. He'd be tempted to take more than she was willing to give.

"You don't want to start now."

"Sounds like the voice of experience."

"It is."

He wanted to say more, to tell her that he respected her and genuinely liked her. There were about five people in the world he felt that way about. But he held his tongue. He wanted her off his mountain so his life could return to normal.

"This area is private property," he said abruptly, wondering if he'd ever behave like a gentleman around her or if he was destined to act like a redneck jerk.

"I'm sorry. I didn't know."

He acknowledged her words with a slight inclination of his head. "Be careful. A dangerous group of men poach up this way. They wouldn't take kindly to finding you here."

"I took a six-week self-defense class."

He doubted that all six weeks' worth of self-defense

would protect her from rowdy rednecks with whiskey on their breath and mischief on their minds. "All the same. I don't want you up here again."

She bent to grab her towel wrapping it around her body, and he breathed sharply through his teeth at the image she presented him.

"Okay. Thanks for the warning."

She gathered her things before pulling on shorts and hiking boots. The expensive kind that exclusive outfitters sold. He watched her leave before heading back to his own hunting, feeling as though his world would never return to normal even after she left because all he could think of was that perfect body in a soaking-wet red suit.

Leaves rustled and the wind played a sweet melody with the tree branches. Miranda had never taken time to enjoy nature. In fact, she'd always avoided the outdoors until her boss, Mark, had challenged her to find out if she could survive outside the business world. Her doctors had warned her that her stress level was too high and that she was approaching the danger zone, but she still hadn't been able to stop working because it was the one area of her life she could control.

Her goal of partner had been obtained, and Warren had broken their engagement. She had run into him at the mall with his new bride. A woman who wanted nothing more than to stay at home and raise a family. A woman who cooked and cleaned and looked forward to keeping the perfect house and supporting her husband's career. A woman, she'd soon realized, that had everything that she, Miranda, wanted for herself. Suddenly her job hadn't seemed so important anymore. She'd wanted—no, needed—a change and she'd found something more.

Luke Romero sparked more than passion in her and a big part of her needed to explore the desire, humor and masculine challenge that he offered.

Her own footsteps echoed on the path and Miranda halted as she heard the sound of a struggle. She followed the noises, not afraid for herself because she'd taken several self-defense classes in the city. She pulled her pepper spray from her bag.

Miranda bit back a scream of protest upon finding a deer caught in a trap. The animal stared at her from deep brown eyes that ironically reminded her of Luke. She went over to the deer and bent to examine the trap. It was old and rusted. She knew nothing about hunting, but knew that she had to hurry before further damage was done to the animal.

The steel jaws were almost impossible for her to open. Without a second thought she screamed. A loud sound straight from her diaphragm that her self-defense instructor had taught her to use if she was attacked. Luke had to be nearby, she thought frantically.

He'd know what to do, how to save this poor defenseless animal. Oh, God. What if he didn't get here in time? What if—

"Miranda, get away from that trap before you get hurt."

"No, I can't leave him here." She hated her husky tone of voice but she couldn't control her outrage.

"I'll take care of it," he said gently.

He walked to her and brushed her hands aside. Her fingers were already scraped and bruised. Deftly Luke opened the steel trap, and freed the deer. The animal scampered away, undeterred by the small injury.

Miranda's hands ached and she wanted to bury her head against Luke's strong chest and cry. She wanted to let him take away this awful image with the beauty of his kiss. She'd thought she'd seen all manner of atrocity on the evening news, but being confronted with the deliberate cruelty of man…

"Why would someone do this?" she asked.

"They can make a clean kill and use the hide. This land

permits rifle or bow-and-arrow hunting only. But because of the remote location, poachers sometimes lay traps.''

He was so close that each word from his mouth brushed across her cheek. He smelled fresh and clean, faintly of a cigar. She forgot about her injured hands.

"Isn't that against the law?" she asked, trying to focus on something other than Luke.

"Yes, but the only punishment for this crime is a fine. Once the fine is paid, the poachers will be back."

He brushed a strand of hair from her face. His touch was warm and inviting, helping to ease her sense of outrage and horror.

"It doesn't seem fair," she said, knowing she sounded like a petulant child but unable to help it.

"I know."

The understanding and promise of retribution in his gaze calmed part of her outrage. Luke wasn't any happier about the situation than she was. But he lived here year-round and knew more about how to deal with the poachers than she did.

"My hands hurt," she said out loud as the pain registered. Though both appendages were scraped, her right hand had sustained a deep gouge from a desperate attempt to free the buck.

Luke lifted them carefully toward his face. The torn flesh along the tips of each finger were treated to a gentle caress. He brushed his lips over her palm. Her heartbeat accelerated and the pain receded in the face of desire.

"Come on. I'll help you back to your cabin. You need to clean and bandage those hands. Have you had a tetanus shot recently?"

"Yes." The walk to her cabin demonstrated how useless she'd be without the use of both hands. She tripped and only Luke's quick reflexes saved her from disaster. Those small touches had made her so physically aware of him that she was clumsier than usual.

She wanted to feel his strong arm around her waist, his fingers on her stomach causing a heavy warmth to pool in her center. She tried to act casually, as if having Luke in her small cabin were a normal thing.

But it wasn't.

"Do you have a first aid kit?" he asked, standing right behind her. She could feel the heat from him along her back. She'd never thought that she was a highly sexed person, but the longer she was in Luke's presence the more she felt she could become one. She wanted to turn around and burrow against his chest, to rise up on her toes and kiss his mouth, to caress his muscled chest—

"Miranda?"

She flushed a little. "Yes, I have supplies."

She directed him to the brand-new kit. He laid the gauze, alcohol and antiseptic cream on the counter. The arrangement of the tools for bandaging her hands was precise. He'd lined everything up in the order it would be used. His attention to detail made her grin.

"Come closer, darlin'."

She both loved and hated his endearment because it made her feel as if she were cherished, and in truth she suspected he used the term with every woman he met. For the time being, she decided to revel in the small feeling of being special to a man. Something she'd never experienced before.

He bent over her left hand cleaning her fingertips and his hair fell forward, brushing against her arms. He shook his head, trying to get the troublesome locks into place. She wanted to grab the silky stuff in both her hands and hold it out of the way for him. To sink her fingers to his scalp and pull his mouth up to hers and experience once again the raw passion in his kiss.

Cool down, Miranda.

"Tell me more about riding cows," she said.

"Not cows, darlin'. Bulls." He filled a medium-size

bowl with warm water and washed her right hand. His experienced touch worked carefully over the injured skin.

She loved his accent. The way that his sentences flowed smoothly in that drawling tone. She let the sound of his voice wash over her.

"There's a difference?" she asked after a few minutes had passed.

He set the bowl aside and picked up the bottle of alcohol and a square gauze pad before answering her question.

"As big as the one between you and me, darlin'."

The look in his eyes reminded her of the way he'd held her last night. The banked fire of desire blazed there and Miranda felt her own blood begin to boil. She wanted to lean closer to him and invite his passion to break free of that steely control of his.

"I've never thought of cattle in sexual terms."

He laughed and smiled at her. One of his rare true grins that made her feel as if she'd just given him a very expensive gift.

"That's good to know. But the bulls have a slightly different perspective on things. This is going to sting," he warned, before dabbing the alcohol onto her palm.

It did sting, but his warm breath bathing over the cuts took her breath away.

"How'd you get into the rodeo circuit?" She forced the question out, needing to focus on something other than Luke.

"My father and I had a falling-out after my marriage fell apart. I had rodeoed in high school so I knew there was some money to be made in it."

His words were steadily spoken, yet she heard a deeper nuance than she'd heard earlier. Before, humor and remembered fun had been dominant. Now…pain?

He applied the antiseptic to her injury.

"You were married?" she asked. The overhead lights reflected off the diamond stud earring. Fascinated by his strong features and hard mouth, she wished he'd kiss her again. She missed his taste and touch.

"I refused to let my wife cuckold me with my brother."

Why would any woman want another man when she had Luke? "What happened?"

"You don't want to know."

"Maybe you need to talk about it."

He paused for a long moment, staring at her as if she'd suggested he should bludgeon himself with a sharp object. "It's supposed to help."

He nodded. "On my son's third birthday I found my wife and brother in bed together."

A son. Oh, God, he had a child. What had happened? Men placed such importance on a continuing genetic line. The flat tone of his voice, completely devoid of the drawling accent she'd come to love, shocked her. Maybe he was right. This was not something she wanted to hear. Already her heart ached for him. For the betrayal he must have suffered at the hands of his brother and wife. Honor, a code that he lived by, would demand that he take retribution against both of them.

"What did you do?"

Luke stopped working on her hands and stared down at her as if he'd forgotten she was there. His face was filled with the type of pain she associated with old men or women who had physical ailments. Despite his anger, he held her hands gently.

"I told her that I wanted a divorce and sole custody of our son." His voice drifted and Miranda knew he was no longer talking to her. She doubted he was even aware of her presence.

"Suzanne explained that Brett wasn't my son, but my nephew, and that she was never parting with Brett.

"I lost it. I hauled my brother out of the bed and punched him. I don't know how far it would've gone if my father hadn't walked in. He pulled us apart and sent everyone to bed.

"Suzanne left in the night, taking Brett with her."

He put the finishing touches on her bandages and cleaned up the mess with efficient motions. Miranda realized he wasn't going to say anymore.

"Why did your father blame you?"

"My brother was running for state senate and I was supposed to pretend that everything was peachy with Suzanne and myself until after the election. But I wouldn't go along with the plan and threatened to take my son and go to the press. And then Suzanne ran off with Brett."

"It was hardly your fault she left."

He glared at her but Miranda knew the anger wasn't directed at her. "No, but when my brother left two days later to find her I told him that I'd never speak to him again."

"Did your brother return home with Suzanne?"

"I heard he did, but not until years after I'd left for good."

"I'm sorry," Miranda said rather awkwardly. She simply didn't know what to say to him. Didn't know how to express her sorrow without sounding like an insensitive person.

"Don't be. I learned an important lesson that day."

"What?"

"Not to trust women, sweetcake."

She reached out to touch him and he sidestepped her arm. Miranda knew she had no right to try to reach beyond the wall of his control, but that didn't stop her from wanting to. Or from aching when she realized that she wouldn't be able to scale the wall. Because the only thing that could possibly heal Luke was to have a son of his own by a woman who was loyal, and that was the one thing she couldn't give him.

Six

Luke's first impulse was to get the hell out of the cabin. Still shaken from Miranda's attempt at freeing the buck, he hadn't been prepared to deal with all the emotional garbage left over from losing his family and home.

He'd never held women in high esteem, but Suzanne's betrayal had been the final straw. Now he faced a bigger emotional upheaval in the form of one small, curvy woman.

Miranda shook him to his core, rocking beliefs he'd held for a lifetime because her innocence was real. She understood what honor was and that once the code was broken you could never go back.

Her high-pitched scream had brought home the fact that she'd begun to matter to him. The storm threatened in the distance, bringing with it colder weather.

He knew with her right hand bandaged there were few chores she'd be able to do on her own. She couldn't fix dinner. Biting back a chuckle, he figured that was no great loss. Intelligent and sexy, Miranda might be, but she couldn't cook worth a damn, if those cookies were any indication.

He scanned the interior of the cabin, stopping on the bed behind her. The wrought iron bedstead and unmade mattress beckoned him closer. The lust which had been his constant companion since their embrace the other night hit him hard.

His blood pooled in his groin and he shifted his stance, trying to relieve some of the pressure. Hell, who was he kidding? He'd wanted her ever since she looked up at him from a sprawl at his feet. A cloud of brown curls surrounding her face and a mixture of embarrassment and outrage in her clear gray eyes.

"Damn," he muttered out loud.

"Luke," she said, her voice soft, husky, brushing over his tingling nerves like a velvet pillow across his skin. He stared at her, but saw her only in his mind. He saw her creamy white skin bared to his gaze. Would her nipples be pink or a darker rose color? Would they respond to his mouth the way they had to the cold or would he have to touch and tease them to readiness with his fingers before he could suckle there as he longed to?

He saw her lying on her back, writhing, those slim curvy legs bare to him. He wanted to sink his fingers into her flesh. To find the place where her legs met and explore her as he'd explored no other woman. To show her all the passion she was capable of.

Yet he needed her to feel safe enough to come to him, and that horny behavior wasn't going to reassure her. Whether she was the vulnerable woman she seemed or if it was just an act, he didn't want her to fear him or his desire.

Cool down, he warned himself. *Take control of this wild thing before it takes control of you.* He needed to distance his emotions from his libido.

He noticed the empty wood box next to her fireplace.

Cold weather could be unpredictable. The mountains were anything but gentle in spring.

"Do you have logs outside for the fireplace?" he asked abruptly, needing to distance himself from her and her unmade bed.

"No. I haven't quite mastered the fine art of wood chopping."

He studied her slender arms and fine-boned hands, wrapped in bandages, before glancing down at his own scarred and callused palms. He existed in a world that she couldn't survive in. There were differences between them that could never be breached.

"There's no great skill involved. Only brute strength is necessary." *His specialty.*

"Somehow I don't think brute strength is going to be my forte," she said wryly.

Luke liked hard physical labor, and juvenile as it may be, he looked forward to impressing Miranda with his prowess at surviving in nature's wilds.

"I'll chop it for you."

"You don't have to."

Her soft breath bathed his face in her scent. A sweet smell that he only associated with Miranda. He'd never identified one particular thing with a woman before her. But now everything about her was etched in his mind.

"I don't mind."

"There you go being kind again."

He kissed her then because she sounded almost sad and he wanted to see her smile. But more than that he needed to taste her. She made his hormones crazy and he didn't want to think about what she did to his emotions.

Her mouth opened on a sigh. Her shy tongue rubbed briefly over his teeth before plunging deeper into his mouth. Luke grunted and pulled her close. Tilting his head, he deepened the kiss.

He caressed her back, down to her curvy bottom and

pulled her against his arousal. *Oh, God, yes.* This was what he needed.

She moaned deep in her throat and moved against him, trying to get closer. He didn't hamper her attempts. She twined her hands in his hair and she held him steady as if fearing he'd leave her.

Yeah, right. He wasn't going anywhere in the foreseeable future—except to the bed across the room.

He pulled her shirt free and at last felt her soft skin. She felt like the misty mornings on the mountain—soft and sweet, making him feel as if he were close to heaven.

She arched her back and he held her closer against his chest. Her breasts brushed against him. For the first time in years he fought to keep his control. This woman went to his head faster than old Edgar's moonshine.

Her nipples were hard, he couldn't resist touching them. He broke their kiss and tasted the long smooth column of her neck. Biting the juncture where her shoulder began. She shivered and moaned—a husky sound of arousal that drove him to the outer limits of his control.

He was so hard right now that it would take the slightest touch of her body to send him over the edge. He thought about it. Thought about her hands on his body and shuddered. Her grip on him tightened. She slid her hands along his back down to his butt, pulling him into closer contact with her woman's body. He couldn't get any closer unless he was inside her.

Her nails flexed, digging into him, holding him where he was while she rocked against him. He lifted her higher, latching on to the hardened nipple through the barrier of her clothing. He suckled strongly needing something more than he was getting from her. Something that she hadn't denied him. Still he wanted more.

The roll of thunder interrupted his single-minded quest to get her naked. Rain started falling, echoing on the old tin roof of the cabin and seeping through holes in the ceiling. The drops shockingly cold against his passion-hot flesh.

Miranda pulled back. Her eyes bright and glossy, her lips red and swollen, her body tense and frustrated.

He cursed. Not the kind of word he usually used in front of a woman but the kind that he used when he dropped a heavy piece of furniture on his toe. Only this felt worse than an injured toe. This interruption he felt to the center of his soul and that scared him. Though he'd never admit it out loud.

"That got out of hand."

This cabin of Edgar's wasn't worth the wood it was made out of, Luke thought with disgust. He helped Miranda place bowls under most of the leaks.

"Thanks," she said softly.

He barely heard her over the drone of the rain and didn't know what she was thanking him for—stopping or starting in the first place. She shivered as a gust of wind blew moisture through the screened door. He crossed the room and closed the door for her.

He'd been thinking that he should let Miranda be her own protector. If he tried to seduce her and she succumbed then it was her responsibility, but he knew now that he couldn't. Somehow she'd begun to matter to him in a way that other women never could.

"Want to stay for dinner?" she asked.

"Yes."

The solid word echoed in the darkness and he realized that he didn't want to leave tonight—maybe first thing in the morning.

Miranda tried to ignore Luke's presence in her small, wet cabin as she set the table. She wished she'd brought her bone china and silver flatware up from Atlanta with her. Sensing that he hadn't had a lot of softness in his life, she wanted to surround him with it. She wanted him to have all the things that he'd once had on his father's ranch but things that he'd never get for himself.

Still reeling from the betrayal he'd suffered at the hands of people who were supposed to love and support him, she wanted to shower him with her caring. And she did care for him in a way that she hadn't cared for her ex-fiancé.

She knew from the healthy, almost overwhelming sensuality that surrounded him that this man had experienced too much of the earthy side of life. She met him on unfamiliar ground and had no advantages at her disposal. She had to find a way to protect herself.

Not because she feared he'd hurt her—not physically. Luke had a code of honor and chivalry that most men never reached. She doubted that it was even a conscious thing. He treated men, women and nature with respect. He expected the same in return.

Preparing dinner was a challenge since her right hand was wrapped in gauze, but she wanted to repay Luke's kindness. He'd warned her about the woods, told her time and again that a city girl had no place on the side of his mountain, but she'd ignored him. The steady pain in her hand paid the price for that foolishness.

A cold Caesar salad was right up her alley of evening meals that were easy to fix. She felt awkward and inept as she scurried around the kitchen trying to find the ingredients she needed. For once she wanted to be competent at the domestic arts, wanted to be a mix between Betty Crocker and Julia Child in the kitchen, wanted to be everything that a man desired in a woman. Wanted to be able to offer Luke everything he needed in a woman, and she knew even if he didn't that what he needed was a child to fill the void in his life left by betrayal.

She remembered the feel of Luke's hand on her shoulder. The rough caress of his callused finger against her own soft skin. She wanted more of his touch, but didn't know how to ask for more. She didn't want to lead him on when she knew with bone-deep certainty that she could never offer him everything a man wanted. If there was one thing that she agreed with Warren on, it was that fact.

But Luke didn't know her faults. He looked at her and saw a woman—not a womb. Warren had only seen her as the bearer of future generations of Markhams.

Without consciously thinking about it, she sought Luke out. He sat on the battered Salvation Army reject couch, looking larger than life.

Afraid to speak, lest he read some nuance in her voice, she moved to the refrigerator, pulling out the romaine lettuce. Her wound throbbed with every beat of her heart. She felt drained—physically and emotionally, as if fixing dinner would sap all the energy she had left. Their earlier embrace left her achy and unsure—afraid to move forward yet wanting to desperately.

"Darlin', do you need some help with that?"

His voice was so tender, she wanted to cry out the injustice of life. This was a man who desperately needed a woman's loving touch in his life. This was a man who bottled his caring, doling it out only in small doses. This man was an outlaw who could steal her heart and break it…or heal it.

She'd once thought that men like Luke didn't exist. That the fabled cowboys of the Old West had been a fairy tale made up by lonely women married to more civilized men. But seeing Luke, sensing the code that he lived very carefully by, she now knew that those men had existed and a handful of lucky women had loved them.

She didn't kid herself. Luke had his faults. She doubted he'd enjoy a performance of the ballet or opera. He preferred living like a hermit on the side of his mountain, but more and more she was beginning to understand that attitude. The peace and solitude of a quiet mist-filled morning soothed the wounds she hadn't realized she'd sustained. Wounds that came from suppressing emotions and working long hours instead of living. Wounds that would heal only if she acknowledged them and faced them.

"This is a low-maintenance meal."

Right up her alley, she thought.

"Really, you should be resting that hand. We don't want you to have any permanent damage," he said before she could speak. He came in to her minuscule kitchen and took the serrated-edge knife from her hand.

He was afraid of her cooking, she realized.

"Luke, I think you're being ridiculous."

"It's better this way. For your health."

And for his. Though he didn't say the words out loud she knew what he was thinking. She started to laugh. He looked a bit apprehensive. "The ingredients for dinner are bottle dressing, romaine lettuce and croutons. I might open a can of soup if I can find the can opener. You're safe."

He relaxed. "I'll take care of the soup."

"You don't want me near the stove."

"No way. After those cookies, I figure combining you and an open flame would be more dangerous than riding bulls."

They settled into a rhythm of quiet camaraderie and finished fixing dinner. She'd tried not to let herself care for Luke Romero. Tried not to let herself believe that this man could accept her as she was. Tried not to let the dreams that she'd carefully hidden from Warren emerge once more.

She dreamed of a family and lifelong happiness with one man. A man who would see her as more than an adornment. A man who could accept her as she was. A man...like Luke. But that was never going to happen.

Seven

Luke prided himself on two things, his honesty and his ability to survive on his own, yet he'd questioned both during the past few days. Miranda's injured hands had rendered her helpless in an environment that showed little mercy on the weak. He knew that she couldn't take care of herself. He *needed* to stop by her ramshackle cabin every day.

At least that's what he told himself.

Honesty finally demanded that he admit he was helping Miranda out because he wanted to. He wanted to be near her, to experience her brand of quiet and understated humor, much like the woman herself. He wanted to see the changes in her expression and watch her drop her guard when something unexpected happened, like seeing a mother bear and her two cubs. He wanted to spend time with her and not necessarily in bed.

That scared Luke almost as much as the newfound feelings unfurling in the pit of his stomach. Somehow or another, when he looked at Miranda, he didn't just see a sexy woman who'd be great in his bed. He saw more. A woman at a crossroad in her life, searching for answers.

Knowing Miranda had decisions to make, Luke took her to his private place for thinking. He wrapped a bandanna around Miranda's eyes, lifting the silky strands of her brown hair out of the way to knot the cloth in place.

"Where are we going?" she asked. He heard the trust in her words—she wasn't afraid of him. That knowledge made his gut tighten and his breathing hard. *No one* had ever trusted him enough to follow him blindly.

"It's a surprise," he said.

He had to get them out of the house or he'd wrap her in his arms and not let go until he'd taken her hard, fast and with the urgency that his body demanded. His self-control would disappear faster than a raindrop on a summer's day. He'd strip both of them of their clothes and make love to her until no other man existed in her memory. That's what all his instincts screamed for him to do. But he couldn't.

She was vulnerable right now. She didn't need some rough man battering at her weakened defenses. Luke sucked in a deep breath and wished he had a cigar. The burn of tobacco against his throat would go a long way in soothing the ills in his life at this moment.

He caressed the back of her hand with his forefinger. Her skin felt so soft. Softer than the first trace of light across the sky at dawn. Softer than anything he'd ever touched. Softer than anyone he'd ever encountered.

He led her out into the darkening twilight. The haunting call of the whippoorwill made him appreciate Miranda's presence. The lonely song of the twilight bird always reminded him of his own life. How he'd chosen to live a life alone, separate from loved ones. Usually it made him wish that things could be different.

But not tonight. Tonight he had the company of a lovely woman.

The tune of the crickets and frogs accompanied them to their destination. The mating call of the hoot owl silenced the bug symphony. Miranda shivered, gripping his hand tighter. "What was that?"

He wondered at the husky note to her voice. Almost as if she were scared. He remembered that she was a city girl. She didn't know a hoot owl from a grizzly and probably didn't have a clue as to what animals were indigenous to the region. "A hoot owl. Nothing to worry about."

"Are we going to the stream?" she asked after a few minutes had passed.

"No." He helped her over a fallen log.

She stopped walking and let go of his hand. "Give me a clue."

He wrapped his hand around her wrist, urging her to keep moving. He wanted to reach their destination before the sun set completely. He had a flashlight in his free hand so they'd have no trouble finding their way back. "If I tell you it won't be a surprise."

"Just a small hint. Even if I guess I'll still be excited."

"Umm."

"What kind of answer is that?" she asked.

"I was thinking."

"Come on. One small clue won't hurt."

"Okay. We're almost there," he said.

"Thanks a lot," she said, but laughter was present in her voice. Her smile stretched wide and he felt as if he'd been sucker punched.

Luke had craved few things in life, preferring to take what the Fates handed him instead of carving out a niche for himself. But he wanted Miranda. He wanted her lusciously curved body in his bed. He wanted the freedom to reach out and caress her when the impulse took him. He wanted to enjoy this wild hunger until it had expired.

The secret bower and hidden meadow were behind the veil of the willow trees. He swept the flowing branches aside and led Miranda through. Wildflowers blanketed the ground. The night air smelled of fresh water and a combination of flower fragrances. Miranda tilted her head back. The warmth of her breath against his neck had the sweet feel of summer's first breeze—hot and tempting.

"Are we there?" she asked, her voice deep and husky.

"Yes. Keep your eyes closed." He placed his hands on her waist, turning her until she faced him.

He reached for the knot at the back of her head feeling her breasts brush against his chest. Her breath rasped against his neck and her hands tightened on his shoulders.

Damn, he thought. He knew there was no way in hell he'd be able to resist this temptation, her body so close to his that he could feel her without really touching. Her lips parted and he could just see the tip of her pink tongue. He leaned in. Every breath he took came from her mouth.

"Oh, darlin', we're in trouble now," he muttered.

Her fingers fluttered up from his shoulder and twisted in the hair at his nape. She pulled at the back of his head until his forehead met hers. Her touch drifted to the hoop earring, then onto his face. She caressed his eyes closed, then moved on to flit briefly over his lips before returning to the back of his head.

"Luke."

He rubbed his mouth against hers with a soft, gentle kiss. He teased the edge of her lips with the tip of his tongue, tasting her sad smile. The one she wore more often than not. He tilted her chin up. "Say no, now."

She shook her head. "I can't."

He brushed his lips against hers and her mouth opened under his. Thrusting his tongue past the barrier of her teeth, he sampled the warm sweetness of her mouth. She moaned deep in her throat and tightened her grip on his neck. He bent to her.

Her small body twisted against his much stronger one with the force of her desire. Never had a woman reacted to him with such honesty. Never had a woman kissed him with such a hunger. Never had a woman's responses been so important to him. He needed her to want him with the same intensity that he wanted her.

He wrapped his arms around her hips and lifted her off the ground. The soft sounds coming from the back of her throat made him want her even more. Never had one kiss affected him this much. Never...

He held her closer, taking her mouth completely. Tasting all of her and more. The essential quality that was Miranda, city girl; savvy and intelligent, but also lost woman. He planned to enjoy all of Miranda and offer all of himself in return at least for the moment. His past made it impossible for him to want more than that. He regretted that Miranda hadn't come into his life earlier when they'd still have had a chance at something more than an affair.

She broke the kiss, gulping in air. He slowly lowered her to the ground, letting her body rub over his arousal. He groaned. God, he wanted her as he'd wanted nothing else in life. He wanted to taste her breasts again. To feel her rocking against his body as she had the other day in the cabin. To bury himself in her and not leave until their senses exploded.

Her grip tightened on his shoulders and she leaned into him rather than pushing away. He removed the bandanna from her eyes and noticed the wild expression in them.

She settled her palm against his cheek, holding his face. The wildness inside Luke still raged. He wasn't ready for her gentleness. Not now while he still pondered the hardness of the ground. His hormones clamored for him to grab her.

"Luke?"

"Give me a minute, darlin'."

Hauling her to his chest, he hugged her close. She kept her hand on his cheek but rested her head right over his heart. He thought he'd forgotten all about the softer emo-

tions like caring and affection but realized suddenly that
they'd only been dormant.

She snuggled her hand into the collar of his shirt. Nest-
ling against him like some small woodland animal. A certain sense of rightness flooded him. Beneath that rightness
was the worry that he could never give her all that she
needed from him. More than mind-blowing sex.

He lifted her, carrying her to the burned out stump of a
tree. He leaned back against the stump and pulled Miranda
closer into the cradle of his body. Her soft curves yielded
to the muscular length of his chest and thighs, fitting perfectly against him. His fingers teased the edge of her shirt,
tugging it free of her waistband.

He ached to feel more of her skin. She sighed and sank
farther into his body. Luke let his fingers wander up her
rib cage to the bounty of her chest.

She stiffened. He stopped moving, letting her get used
to the feel of his hands on her skin. God, she felt so soft
and fragile, making him feel big and awkward. Her accelerated heartbeat throbbed beneath his touch. He sensed that
she wanted his fingers on her.

She trusted him…not to hurt her…to stop this wild thing
before it took control of them both.

Earlier he'd thought her trust in him was misplaced. Now
he knew that his opinion was correct. This woman
shouldn't trust someone like him. She shouldn't be that
honest with him either. She shouldn't let him see how much
he affected her emotions.

Luke wanted to tell her not to trust him. Not to believe
in the false comfort that he offered. After telling her about
his ex-wife and the son that wasn't his biologically, he
knew she'd softened even more toward him. He needed to
make her understand that life often played tricks on those
who believed in happy endings.

Hell, she should already know that, the tough corporate
executive that she was. But he knew that she still believed

in happily ever after. The light in her eyes just moments ago confirmed it. He wanted to tell her what a desperado he really was, but couldn't. Not at this one moment.

She glanced over her shoulder, meeting his gaze squarely. "I…"

"What is it?"

"No man has ever treated me this kindly," she said, putting her hands over his and moving it up to cover her breast.

Oh, hell. *She's offering herself to me.*

"Don't trust me, Miranda."

"Why not?"

"Because everyone who's ever placed their trust in me has regretted it."

"Luke—"

"Look over there."

Luke watched as she turned away from him, disappointment in her expression. He didn't bring her here for an intense discussion, but to show her the twilight show of sun and the nightly bathing of nature's critters. And to let her find her own healing and peace the way he had. He repeated the words again in his head, pushing her away. He needed the distance. More than physical, so much more than mental.

Miranda followed Luke out of the meadow shortly after sunset. The display of color combined with the shadows of the mountain had been a beautiful show. She'd never seen anything quite like it. In fact, she couldn't remember the last sunset she'd seen.

But her thoughts dwelled on Luke's comment.

Because everyone who's ever placed their trust in me has regretted it.

How could he doubt himself on that level? She tried to ignore the burning need to ask him a myriad of questions. His earlier embrace had touched something she'd thought she'd lost. Some frozen place deep inside her. The same place that overhearing her father's remark that she'd never be able to marry since she couldn't have kids had wounded long ago. A weakness she preferred not to admit she still had.

Luke walked so fast she could barely keep the pace. Not that she feared getting lost. Luke's code of honor would not allow him to leave her alone in the woods. A few minutes later they were back at her house, and she knew that Luke planned to leave without saying another word to her. She wondered at the fact that a man with a strict code would doubt his own trustworthiness.

"Luke?" she called as he walked away from her.

He stopped but didn't turn to face her. She continued moving until she stood directly behind him. His sudden withdrawal hurt her deep inside. She wouldn't have guessed that Luke had imbedded himself so permanently into the fabric of her life, but he had.

She cared for him.

"Won't you face me?" she asked, daring him to meet her gaze.

He glanced over his shoulder. "What?"

The gruff tone of his voice intimidated her a bit. She wasn't sure how Luke would react.

"I want to know what you meant earlier," she said softly.

"Leave it alone, darlin'. That's one kettle of fish that's already been fried." He thrust his fingers through his hair and tilted his head toward the darkening sky.

Something had set it off this evening. A comment or action from her had struck some chord of his past. Perhaps she could fix whatever it was that troubled him.

"I can't let it be."

"I don't understand why not," he said, his voice a low rasp in the evening noise. She could barely hear the words, yet she felt them in her heart. She wanted to touch him, but the stiff stance of his body discouraged her.

"Because friends help each other when they are troubled."

He grunted.

She grunted back and saw a half smile tease the corner of his mouth. "Whatever it is will seem lighter when it's shared."

He stepped back, the smile leaving his face. "No, it won't."

"I don't understand."

"I know that. It's better this way."

He laughed after his last words, a harsh brittle sound that made her flinch.

"I *do* trust you."

"Well, don't, darlin'. I only want one thing from a woman and it doesn't involve those lofty ideals that are running through your head. I don't believe in love or even caring. I believe in things that can be felt and seen. I believe in lust and desire, and right now, baby, I want you."

She regretted asking him to explain himself. She felt as if every emotional mooring inside her soul was being ripped to shreds once again. The one thing he wanted from her was the one thing she really wasn't good at. The one thing she couldn't give a man because he would be so damn disappointed in her.

Sex. Why was it so important to men? They seemed to think about it every hour of the day. Heck, since meeting Luke she thought about making love constantly. But making love was different than sex, and she wasn't sure that she could fulfill Luke the way he needed to be. Why couldn't he be satisfied with friendship and caring?

But then that wasn't enough for her anymore.

She liked Luke's hands on her body and his lips pressed against hers. She liked the liquid fire that heated her blood and gave her an adrenaline rush. She liked having his mus-

cled chest brush against her breasts. But she was afraid of
that same reaction.

Maybe she could buy a book that would help her. She
made a mental note to check into that tomorrow when she
went into town.

"I think you're selling yourself short," she said into the
silence that had spread around them.

He stepped toward her, gripping her chin in an inescap-
able grasp. He forced her face toward his. "I'm a cold,
heartless bastard who has always cared for his own comfort
and pleasure above everyone else's."

She blinked back the tears she could feel burning in her
eyes. She wouldn't let him see how much his words hurt.
He wasn't a bastard. Why couldn't he see that?

The lonely caged-wolf look in his eyes made her heart
weep. Oh, damn. It wasn't fair that she should be this vulnerable to him. He didn't feel a damn thing for her. *Not
one thing.*

She couldn't believe she'd let this happen again. She'd
vowed to never let a man lead her down the path to de-
struction. Down into the emotional maelstrom of caring
but...

It was too late.

She stared at Luke in the wavering light of the moon.
His expression had turned grim in the past few moments.
He didn't want her in his life. He wanted her in his bed.

The words echoed in her mind like the sound of a car-
ousel melody, playing over and over again, vaguely familiar but not recognizable. "Luke, I can't give—"

"Listen, darlin'. I know that a woman like you expects
more from a man than the simple pleasures in life. More
than a physical joining so intense that it sets the night on
fire. More than I have to offer. But that is all that I'm
offering you."

She wanted to agree but knew better. She shook her head

and started to speak, but his fingers on her lips stilled the words.

"I can't be around you and not act on this."

In that moment, Miranda had no choice but to react as honestly as he had. "I don't believe that any man could want me like that."

Without another word he lifted her. "Let me show you something."

He carried her into the darkened house and laid her on the bed. He opened the drapes to the window, letting the moonlight flow into the room and fill it with dappled illumination. He reached out, caressing her hair, her cheek and her neck with a tenderness she knew he'd deny.

Bending, he took her mouth in a kiss that left no secrets between them. He used his mouth to tempt the passionate woman she'd hidden beneath the surface of the shy, controlled CPA that Miranda was during the day. She lifted her arms, trying to pull him closer.

But Luke resisted. This wasn't for him. This was to show her how hot things really were between them. To show her how much she turned him on. To teach her that she was more woman than most men could handle.

He gripped her wrists and lifted them to the iron bedstead. "Hold on here, darlin'."

Her eyes were wide and unsure but she tightened her fingers around the bar as he'd instructed.

He bent to kiss her again. This time letting his hands roam down her body. He unbuttoned the prim camp shirt she wore but made no move to bare her to his view. He wanted—no, needed—to make sure that she was with him every step of the way.

Her pulse raced under his mouth, accelerating like a leaf in a windstorm tossed out of control. His mouth roamed farther down her body, tasting the skin revealed by the inch of gaping cloth. She moaned, a deep husky sound that made his blood pool in the center of his body.

"Darlin'?"

"Please."

Using his teeth he pealed the shirt away from her body, seeing her nipples thrust against the lace of her bra. Miranda's lush body was built to be worshiped. Her full breasts beckoned him closer and he ran his forefinger over both distended nipples.

Her tiny waist was no larger than his one hand and he bent to nip at the firm flesh above her waistband. Her hips flared out again. Miranda was the type of woman that all men dreamed of having in their beds. But she didn't believe that.

He reached beneath her and removed her bra. The tightened tip of her breast was a pretty pink color that reminded him of the pearly rays of dawn. He touched her reverently, afraid to frighten her away.

Her hands left the bedstead to cover her breasts. He leaned down to kiss her once again and her arms encircled his shoulders pulling him closer. The rasp of her hardened nipples against his chest made his groin tighten even more. He couldn't stop. He wanted her with an intensity that equaled nothing he'd ever wanted before. All the women in his past faded until, when he thought of a woman, Miranda was all he saw.

He left her mouth to suckle, lick and gently bite the flesh of her breasts. His hand wandered down her body to encounter the rough fabric of her jeans. He unfastened them and rested his hand against the flat surface of her stomach and abdomen.

He dipped his hand lower. Letting his fingers touch the place where she was most a woman.

He wanted to taste her. To explore the honeyed warmth that he'd felt on his fingers moments earlier.

She stiffened. He froze not wanting to frighten her.

"Luke, wait."

He paused looking up at her. She covered her naked chest and took a deep breath. "I've never done this before."

Eight

Luke paused above her, his dark eyes intent and brooding in the dim light of the moon, reminding her of the hawk tattooed on his back. A vulnerability unlike any she'd ever experienced before struck her. Her confession had stripped away barriers she hadn't even realized were there. Barriers that she'd hidden behind for years.

Her body still hummed with satisfaction from his touch. But because she wasn't going to tell Luke that she couldn't have children, she felt she needed to be honest with him in every other way. She'd also had a moment of fear, once she let this man into her body, she'd never be able to erect barriers against him again.

She grabbed for the quilt to cover her exposed torso. He braced his hands on either side of her head and brought his chest down on top of hers effectively covering her nudity. But the feel of the muscled strength tantalized instead of comforted her.

"So there's no more confusion—never had an affair or never taken a man into your body?"

She stared into his chocolate brown eyes and couldn't think for a minute. She'd never been this close, this intimately pressed to a man. She felt his chest move slowly with each inhalation of breath, felt each beat of his heart, felt his hardness pressed intimately against her own femininity.

"I can't think straight when you touch me," she said. Not that it excused letting him go as far as he had.

He arched one eyebrow at her.

It was now or never, she thought. The passionate side of her engagement had never heated up, and she'd told Warren about her untouched state over cappuccino and biscotti. Some very important elements changed when you lay breast-to-chest with an aroused man.

She closed her eyes, preferring to reveal one of her inner secrets without meeting his gaze. "Never been with a man."

His lips touched her brow with the lightest kiss, making her feel special and cherished instead of out-of-date and awkward. The moment could have gone badly, in fact she expected it to. "Open your eyes."

She did. The intensity in his gaze hadn't changed. She blushed, unable to help the flood of embarrassment sweeping through her.

"Why'd you wait so long?" he asked.

She closed her eyes. Lying was easier when you didn't have to look the person in the eye.

"It wasn't a matter of waiting. I've been busy with work and, well, I was engaged once and my fiancé liked the idea of a bride who was really untouched."

She looked at him again once the words were out. Maybe he'd take them at face value and not probe for the real reason. She didn't want Luke to think of her as half a woman.

"What happened to your fiancé?" Luke asked after long moments had passed.

"We wanted different things from our marriage."

"What type of things?"

"He wanted to have kids and thought I should stay home with them. I wanted to keep working." The words were more than a lie, more than the truth, and so much less than she should be telling him.

He levered himself off of her and grabbed the end of the quilt, tossing it over her naked chest.

"Why me?" he asked.

She struggled to explain. The reason she was a virgin was tied so closely in her mind to the fact that she couldn't conceive a child. "It's not like I've been saving myself for some ideal man to come along. You're the first man I've ever wanted to have touch me."

"Darlin', you could do so much better than me. So much better than a burned-out ex-cowboy who makes furniture for a living."

Her throat ached with the need to comfort him. She hated to hear him downgrading himself. He had no idea how appealing he was to her. Because of all of his supposed faults she wanted him all the more.

She tugged her shirt up her arms, pulling the edges across her naked breasts. She tried to fasten it and found that she'd put it on inside-out. She clutched the lapels together.

"Miranda, there are a few things you should know about me."

"Yes," she said, pretending not to notice the shaky tone of her own voice.

She knew that Luke didn't want any ties. It was plain enough from the way he lived, but still, he had a depth of caring that challenged her. She wanted to find a way to bring out all of that caring, find a way to show him how to love. Yeah, right, she thought with sudden cynicism, she, who'd never formed a lasting bond with anyone, wanted to show this man how to love.

"I'll never be able to offer you more than the rest of the summer."

She nodded, feeling as if she'd lost something rare. She understood why he wanted a short-term affair. He must have sensed her flaw. She couldn't expect more from him or any man other than an affair. But would she be content with just one summer?

Already she felt as if she were half in love with him. And it scared her. Emotional involvement carried with it a price that she didn't want to pay. Warren's desertion had hurt her, but Luke could damage her, in a way she didn't think she'd ever recover from.

"I...I thought we could be friends."

There she'd said it. Maybe they could settle into a nice, friendly relationship. They could spend time together without the sexual undercurrents. But she doubted she'd ever stop wanting him. There was something so appealing about his deep brown eyes and long dark hair. Something that called on the most primitive of her instincts, making her want to mate with him.

But she mustn't. He'd need a child of his own to fill the gap left by the betrayal of his brother and ex-wife. And she couldn't give him one.

His eyes narrowed and he tilted his hips to the side in a posture that was blatantly sexual. "We can't ever be friends."

"Why not?"

"We have nothing in common. You're a city girl, born and bred, and I'm a redneck."

"What about this?" She gestured to the bed and her own disheveled appearance.

"The uncontrollable passion between us is a raging fire that will, in time, burn itself out. Passion never lasts for long but while it does, it's hotter and more intense than anything else you've ever experienced. That's what I was trying to say to you earlier. Take a chance on me, baby."

She watched him in the quiet of the room. Luke was the kind of man she'd fantasized about as a teenager. The bad boy that her father would never have let her date, but that she'd always longed to go out with.

He turned to leave, pausing at the door to glance back at her.

"I can't go on like this. I've never wanted a woman the way I want you. Either you come to me as my lover or you stay away from me until you leave. Your choice."

The morning sky was dusted with only a few clouds, beckoning Luke outside. He donned his business suit with the usual feelings of apprehension. *As if he were an impostor.*

He hadn't had a decent night's sleep since he left Miranda a week ago with that ultimatum of his. Images of her bare body and that old-fashioned bed taunted him. He wanted her. Forcing a decision out of her probably hadn't been the smartest thing he'd ever done. But he couldn't keep on this way, in a constant state of arousal.

He pulled his long hair into a ponytail at the back of his neck, leaving the battered Stetson on the nightstand. He changed his hoop earring for the diamond stud. After checking his string tie in the mirror, he headed out.

He'd delivered the last shipment of tables, cabinets and rocking chairs to the small but expensive shop in Asheville the first day Miranda arrived. He'd avoided her like the plague, hoping he'd be able to get past the need to protect that woman, the need to be more to her than he'd ever been to any woman, the need to let her be so much more to him.

But he hadn't. Remembering the taste of her on his lips, the wet heat of her mouth made his groin tighten. But more than desire, it brought all the gentle feelings he'd tried to hide out in the open. The ones that were weaknesses in his soul.

The lust laced with caring, the desire to both ravish and cherish her. Something wild and untamed had flared between them and she was a virgin. That was what had driven him to throw down a challenge before leaving. He'd never been *good*, but he refused to take the final step that would banish him to hell for eternity. Somehow taking Miranda's innocence and offering nothing in return but pleasure didn't feel right.

He wanted to offer her more but couldn't. He'd made a vow to himself a long time ago. Every decision he'd made led him to the top of this mountain for one reason. He couldn't trust his own instincts. More than one woman had used him in the course of his life and he didn't want to have to lump Miranda in with the bunch when she left.

Luke pulled up to the stop sign at the bottom of his mountain. A small, battered green Mercedes sat on the side of the road. He knew that car. A brief glance at the shadowy interior confirmed the sports car was empty.

It wasn't his problem.

All he had to do was turn west, away from the town of Jessup Springs. He wouldn't even drive past her. He scanned the horizon and found Miranda walking at her usual brisk pace toward town.

He signaled and started toward the highway before slamming on the brakes and making a U-turn. Aside from the fact that she was a woman and therefore deserving of his help and protection—something he knew would make her bristle—he *had* to help her.

Miranda was the one person in this world who'd listened to him and not ridiculed him. The one person who'd taken the time to thank him for something that he considered his duty. The one person who made him remember what it felt like to be alive. Really alive, not just playing at it the way he'd done in the past.

He was angry at himself and, perversely, at this woman. Miranda had respected his evasion and kept to herself as well. No more baskets of overbaked cookies or fresh-picked berries appeared on his front porch. In fact, she'd even stayed away from the stream where he'd once caught her bathing.

He should drive by. He should speed up and pretend that he didn't recognize the car or the woman. But he couldn't.

He idled up behind her. Instead of stopping, Miranda hurried her pace. Damn fool woman, he thought.

Reaching across the empty seat, he rolled down the window. "Miranda?"

"Go away," she said without looking up at him.

Luke toyed with the notion of doing just that. Seeing her reminded him of all he'd been trying to forget. Reminded him of the heat that had spilled from her body onto his hand. Reminded him that her hips were softly curved and made to wrap around his hips. Reminded him that he needed to be buried hilt deep in her body.

Her slim legs, revealed by the short billowing skirt, made his fingers tingle with the need to caress them, to slide his palm up under the gauzy material—

"No," he said to both his thoughts and the woman standing there.

She sighed, a broken, lonely sound that made his defensive anger disappear. He pulled onto the shoulder in front of her, watching in the rearview mirror.

Miranda stood with her arms crossed over her chest and her head bowed. She looked utterly defeated. Luke climbed slowly out of the Suburban. He approached her carefully.

"What is it? What's wrong?"

"Why do you always have to be the one to rescue me?" she asked.

"I..."

"Don't bother trying to answer that. I really don't want to know."

Her dejected behavior worried him. The Miranda he knew didn't get discouraged when things weren't going her way. She hitched up her belt and manipulated the events until she was in control.

"I'll give you a ride to town."

"No, thank you."

"Ah, hell, darlin'. Come on."

"Don't cuss at me, Luke Romero. You're the one who told me to stay away unless..."

He bit back the instinctive swear word, knowing better than to use it now. "This is an exception."

Yeah, right. He wanted her so badly at this moment that his hands shook. And he could see that she wanted him, too. She edged away from him as he reached out for her.

He felt like a complete heel. What kind of man told a woman to stay away unless she wanted to sleep in his bed and then hassled her about accepting his help? He felt like the lowest scum of the earth.

But he wouldn't leave her here. Sure, Jessup Springs was a small town, but he didn't like the thought of Miranda at some stranger's mercy.

"I'm not leaving you here alone."

"I don't see why not. After all, I'm a big 'city' girl."

His temper boiled and more than anything he wanted to channel that anger into passion. To use it as an excuse to go to her and ravish her sullen lips. To force that cold expression from her thin face.

"Stop quoting my words back to me. If I were stranded, would you drive by?"

"Yes."

Her answer surprised him.

She sighed a heavy, haunted sound. "But then I'd have to come back and help you."

His heart lightened. He reached for her hand, but wisely, she stepped away, walking to the truck without his help.

She climbed into the passenger seat of the Suburban. He

started the engine and the five-minute drive into town was conducted in silence. He parked at the service station and waited while Miranda went inside. He knew that if he walked in there with her, Mr. Hammings would expect him to answer all of the questions about the car.

Miranda, staunch little feminist that she was, would probably knock old Henry back on his chauvinistic butt. Luke allowed himself his first real smile of the day. He glanced down at his watch, realizing how much time had passed since he'd left his cabin. He had to be in Asheville in less than an hour. He'd give Miranda another ten minutes before searching her out.

She returned before the thought was fully formed. She walked up to the driver's side.

"The tow truck is at an accident on the highway."

He waited, knowing she wanted something from him.

"I…I wondered if you'd be able to tow the Mercedes into town for me."

"I'd love to, darlin'. But I've got an appointment to get to."

She bit her lip, reaching into her purse for her sunglasses. The large designer frames dominated her face, blocking her eyes from his view. What was she thinking?

"Want to ride with me?" he asked. What the hell was he thinking?

"You don't mind?" she asked hesitantly.

"Hell, I wouldn't have asked if I did."

She seated herself next to him without another word, and he berated himself the entire drive to Asheville.

"Civilization, at last," Miranda muttered under her breath as they drove through the small but picturesque town. She stared out the window at the buildings they passed.

Luke bit back a savage curse. She'd just confirmed what he already knew. She had no place on his mountain or in his life. If he took her to bed, and he wanted to more than he wanted his next breath, then he had to get past this…caring.

Luke unloaded the large, blanket-wrapped parcels from the back of the truck. Miranda noticed the way his jacket tightened, as his muscles flexed to lift the bundles. The tension following him all morning seemed to intensify now that they were in the city. She knew he disliked crowds but hadn't realized how much. Even if Luke could face a childless future, their life-styles were too different for him to be happy with her and her way of life.

"Can I help?" she asked, climbing out of the truck.

"Sure," he said, shrugging out of his suit jacket and handing it to her.

"Gee, I feel really important now," she muttered. "Kind of like a gopher."

"Later you can fetch me some water," he said with a sexy wink.

"Later you can take a flying leap into the lake."

The bold sound of his laughter filled the loading dock and echoed long after he'd disappeared into the building. Curious about the large parcels, Miranda stepped closer to the back of the truck. Peering over her shoulder to confirm that Luke hadn't returned, she lifted a corner of the blanket.

"What are you doing?" Luke asked, his voice seeming to come out of nowhere.

Miranda turned with her hand at her throat. "You scared me."

"Good," he said, with a hint of his usual teasing self.

"What are you doing here?"

"Conducting business." He flushed a bit and grabbed another of the bundles.

Miranda followed him up the loading dock and into an empty storage room. He set the bundle on the floor and turned to face her. "What are you doing in here?"

"Following you."

"Miranda," he said. His voice held a warning.

"I want to know what type of business you're conducting."

"Why?"

"I'm a shrewd negotiator. I could help you."

He chuckled. "I have no doubt that you are. But I can take care of myself."

"Okay." Miranda started back to the truck, only to be stopped by his hand on her arm. He brushed one finger against the side of her cheek, and a shiver of sensual delight coursed through her. She really had to stop reacting to his every touch. It would be nice if her body listened to her mind. But she knew that wouldn't happen any time soon.

"I'm delivering furniture."

"Handcrafted?"

Clearly uncomfortable discussing his business, Luke tugged at his lobe and nodded.

Miranda stepped past Luke, approaching the first blanket-covered bundle. "Can I take a peek?"

"Sure."

Miranda untied the rope that held the blanket in place. The cloth dropped to the floor revealing a beautifully made pine rocker. Small details had been carved into the back of the chair. The woodland scene depicted took her breath away.

"How'd you get started in carpentry?"

"My granddad taught me to whittle and do woodwork. When I retired from the rodeo it was the only thing I wanted to do. Up here I'm my own boss and I don't have to be confined in an office without a view."

She uncovered the rest of the bundles, finding a set of cabinets and a coffee table.

"They're wonderful."

He flushed and looked away. "It keeps food on my plate."

But it didn't really. Luke kept food on his table by hunting and living off nature. This just gave him the means to stay isolated on his mountain, and while she wanted him with a desire unlike anything she'd ever experienced before, she knew with bitter certainty that he'd never leave the safety of his mountain.

Nine

Nine

Miranda felt the world narrow to only the two of them as she watched him bend to examine the bottom of one of his exquisite rocking chairs. He had a nice butt, she thought with a grin. She wasn't in the habit of noticing those types of things but something about his backside appealed to her.

Since coming to North Carolina she'd realized several things had been missing in her life. Luke seemed to exemplify all of those things. Most particularly his love of nature, his moody harmonica music and his love of wood reminded her of the pleasure in simple things.

Some indefinable thing shifted inside her, as though a carnival mask were being torn from her face. The truth was suddenly revealed to her. She loved him.

Oh, God, no.

She wrapped her arms around her middle and turned blindly for the door. Needing to be anywhere but there. Needing to be far away so that she could try to shove that emotion back behind the wall where she'd hidden it. Needing to remind herself of all the reasons why she couldn't let herself love this man.

Luke was ten times more dangerous to her than Warren had been. Her ex-fiancé hadn't looked beyond the superficial barriers she'd erected. Luke already reached into her soul, and they were nothing more than friends. *Very intimate friends.*

She paused on the loading dock, the smell of diesel fumes and cigarette smoke clouding her fervent hopes for some sort of divine intervention. Some sort of answer from above that would help her make the right choice. What choice was there, really? she demanded of herself.

She could seduce the most interesting, caring man she'd ever met—the man she loved—or she could continue living her life in a cold, unemotional state. But there was the issue of fear again. She wondered if there was a book on seduction and realized that there were probably many. Should she pick one up?

She twisted her fingers together, nervous in a way she'd never been before. No one in her life had ever touched her the way Luke did. He forced his way into her soul so completely, evoking feelings that ravaged her heart, leaving her quivering on the brink of something special.

Luke strode down the ramp, straight toward her. He was breathtakingly handsome in his tailored suit. He reached up to pull the rubber band from his hair and loosened his tie simultaneously. The long, thick mane of midnight-colored hair waved behind him. His tanned neck, revealed by his open collar, made her fingers itch to touch him.

She wanted that wild man—that outlaw—in her bed. How much longer could this go on? The wanting and not having. The needing and not acknowledging.

She knew he was right. The two of them should stop talking, visiting and fishing together. The only real solution to the attraction was to back away from each other. Or they'd burn each other alive.

"You okay?" he asked. His deep voice reached out and soothed her troubled thoughts.

"Yes. I wanted to leave you to your business."

"I thought you were going to protect me," he said, a wry grin touching his face.

Knowing that she wanted him but could never have him sliced a deep wound through the very core of her soul. "Since when do you need protection?"

He cursed under his breath and stalked down the ramp to the truck. Anger marked every step he took.

Miranda hated herself for the hard cutting words, her anger self-directed. "Luke, wait."

He paused.

"I...I didn't mean it that way."

His boot heels rang against the concrete as he crossed back to her. As usual he came close enough for her to feel his breath against her face. She reached out to touch his arm, removing a piece of imaginary lint.

"What did you mean?" he asked, his voice huskier than usual.

"To remind myself of something."

"What?"

She forced herself to meet his gaze. She wanted—no needed to deal with him as honestly as he'd always dealt with her, because she knew she'd never tell him she couldn't have kids. "A lesson I learned a long time ago."

He stared into her eyes for a long minute. His brown gaze heavy and intense. Miranda felt like a piece of wood that he was thinking of making into one of his prized rocking chairs. A work in progress that would yield its secrets to only him. She didn't like that comparison even it if was her own.

"Now do you understand why I told you to stay away, darlin'? There are too many undercurrents between us."

There was too much between them. She wanted to argue with him, to tell him that she'd changed her mind. She followed him to his truck. He held the door for her and helped her onto the seat with a hand above her elbow.

His heat burned through the silk of her shirt. She could feel the rough calluses on his palm. They were so different, she thought, in more ways than one.

She wanted to feel his work-hardened hands on her skin again. The back of his fingers brushed against the side of her breast. Her nipples tightened as she remembered the last time he'd touched her. Her blood seemed as thick as molasses, moving slowly through her veins and pooling at her pulse points.

His hand slid from her elbow down to her wrist and she shivered. Never had desire for a man been so strong that every part of her soul wanted to ignore common sense and wallow in it...in him.

"Miranda?"

She'd been standing there, staring at the open door of the truck. She watched Luke walk around the Suburban. He moved smoothly like a man secure in his place in the world, but he wasn't. Luke had so much emotional baggage after the loss of his family, especially his son/nephew. Her presence on the mountain made it worse for him.

He opened the door and slid behind the wheel. She stared at the strength in the motion.

"What?" he asked.

The abrupt question made her want to smile. Luke had no pretenses unlike the other men she'd known—men who dealt daily in half-truths and evasions. Her emotions for him no longer baffled her. She loved him because she trusted him to never lie to her. Something every man she'd ever known had done, even her father whom she respected more than any man...until now.

"Nothing," she said, glancing away.

He drove around the front of the furniture store, pulling on his sunglasses. "Want to grab some lunch after we tow your car into town?"

"No," she said, needing time to come to terms with these new feelings. Time to make plans and decisions. Time to battle her fear.

He stared at her for a moment before turning away. "Whatever you say, darlin'."

The cold tone cut to her heart. She'd hurt him without meaning to. "Luke, it's not as if—"

He touched her lips, stopping the nervous flow of words. "I know. I just wish it could be different. But a woman like you will always need more than I can give."

Not true, she thought. She had less than a man would want and Warren had told her that a woman like her couldn't be choosy.

He brushed his thumb across her bottom lip. The sweet abrasion made her insides clench. She sighed and his finger stilled. Miranda watched in amazement as his dark brown gaze deepened with the light of desire.

Unable to help herself, she sucked his finger into her mouth and caressed it. He tasted slightly salty and so utterly masculine that she froze. Unsure of herself and what she was doing, she flushed and pulled away from him.

She'd been burned too badly in the past to throw caution to the wind. But he made her forget to be cautious.

Luke tightened the tow bar to the back of the Suburban before attaching the cable to the battered Mercedes. The car and its lady looked overtired, both at the edge of their endurance. The car from overuse, but the lady...ah, hell, the blame for her exhaustion lay solely on his shoulders. She'd seemed tired and weary when she arrived on his mountain. Her vacation hadn't allotted her any rest. Just the emotional and sexual turmoil of an attraction that neither of them had expected, but one too powerful to ignore.

He yearned to offer her comfort. To wrap her in a big bear hug—to simply hold her until the confusion in her eyes disappeared, until she wore a smile instead of a frown. But he knew that he wanted to give her more than solace.

Miranda brought out more than sexual desire in him. She made him want to prove that he was a good provider, that he could clothe her, shelter her and protect her. But the past had taught him that the things he wanted the most were the very things he shouldn't have.

He'd wreaked nothing but disaster on his family by indulging in his temper and saying things he shouldn't have said. Threatening to take Brett, the nephew he'd believed was his son, and leave. Threatening to ruin Jake's senate bid by telling the press the whole sordid truth. Threatening to hurt his family the way they'd hurt him.

His father had died before Luke had made his peace with the old man and now his brother, his ex-wife and nephew lived at the ranch as he'd always thought to.

"Dammit," he cursed under his breath. The fierce desire for Miranda would lessen in time or with familiarity, he told himself, but the past spoke of a pain that wouldn't lessen. No matter what happened with Miranda, a part of him would always want her.

Why did it feel like someone had ripped his heart out when he thought of her off his mountain and back in her city? The muscle languishing from years of neglect now seemed ready to explode with life. A gaping wound opened in his soul, hurting him in a way he'd hoped never to be hurt again. He knew then that these emotions weren't meant to be.

It shouldn't feel like this—not because of a woman. He could understand how losing his son, the horses, the ranch hurt like a rusty blade. But to suffer because of Miranda was something he'd never thought would happen.

These feelings coming because of a woman were as shocking as a knife in the back. Never before had a woman affected his thoughts so thoroughly. Physical desire took him as far in his relationships as he wanted to go. He preferred the cold calculating women whom he'd tangle with in the past. Preferred the emotions that they'd left lying dormant deep inside him. Preferred... Oh, hell. The only thing he really preferred was Miranda.

And he'd run her off.

Scared the lady but good. It was for the best. Sharing intimacies with a woman whom he cared for would leave him vulnerable. Especially when she left—and he knew she'd leave.

He wasn't sure he wanted her to stay. Not really. A woman as caring as Miranda deserved all that life had to offer, and that included children and a husband. The role of father and spouse was one he wouldn't commit himself to. Not after Suzanne.

"You okay?" she asked.

Her gray eyes were tinged with concern. *For him.* Oh, hell. Why couldn't she be a woman who used manipulation as Suzanne had? His defenses weakened when faced with the innocent, guileless consideration in her gaze. "Yeah."

"I really appreciate your taking the time to do this."

He shrugged off her gratitude, her manners niggling under his skin. Not so much because of the propriety, but because of the prim and proper tone she used to deliver them. As if he were nothing more to her than a stranger. And he was so much more. Whether she acknowledged it or not, they'd never be strangers again. "What's to appreciate? I couldn't leave you stranded at Hammings Garage all afternoon waiting for a tow."

"Why not?"

The quick aversion of her gaze told him that she regretted asking the question. That the words had slipped out without her intending them to. He liked pushing her beyond the confines of what she knew was proper.

His hunger for her leapt out beyond the boundaries of his control. He wished there was a way to demonstrate just why he found it impossible to ignore her. A way to show her what he meant that she'd understand.

Instead she stood by the side of the road with her arms crossed protectively around her waist. The arousal he'd been fighting all day sprang to pulsing demand. He paced toward her, not stopping until less than a breath separated them.

She smelled like the mountains after a spring rainstorm, the scent teased him as much as her body did. The soft exhalation of her breath brushed against his neck. He reached out, placing his hands on her shoulders.

She flinched, but she didn't back up. *Not Miranda Colby.* This stubborn woman held her ground like an Amazon defending her tribe. But she wasn't an Amazon, she was a virgin who was probably more than a little scared of the overwhelming male in her face.

He released her abruptly. He didn't want to frighten her. Yes, he wanted to push her away from him so that he wouldn't be tempted by her sexuality, but he didn't want her afraid of him.

"Luke, why are you doing this?" she asked, but curiosity more than confusion laced her words.

Because I'm a bastard, he thought. Maybe scaring her would finally drive her away from him before he did something foolish—like fall in love with her. She thought she understood how he felt, women always did. Reading a book on the differences in brain chemicals between the sexes and watching talk shows wasn't going to help any woman understand him, especially Miranda.

"You wanted a reason for why I'd help you, didn't you?" The words were harsh, having been forced through his dry throat. All he could think about were her lips, full and peachy pink, so close that if he leaned in, he could taste them. The feel of her curvy little body pressed against his wouldn't leave him. He wanted her in his arms again and this time he wasn't stopping no matter what.

"You're helping me..."

"Because I can't drive past you and not stop. Because I need to make sure you're as safe as I can make you." He covered her mouth when she started to speak. "Because you're the only person who's ever baked me cookies."

He dropped his hand and backed away. He hadn't meant to reveal so much. Those cookies of hers had started a spark of caring that was slowly growing into a blaze out of control.

Luke knew then that he wasn't going to try to scare her off his mountain. He was going to try and make her stay, any way he could. Because if she left, he'd lose something he only just found.

She hesitated, clearly not sure what to do. She nibbled her lower lip before nodding.

He tracked the motion and felt his already straining body tighten even more. Dammit, he'd already decided to slow down. Why the hell didn't his groin get the message?

His arguments served to heighten the precipice he was hovering over. He wanted to lean down and take the soft flesh of her lower lip between his own teeth. To suckle and tease her mouth until she opened for him, allowing him to taste her inner sweetness.

"Luke?" she said after he didn't speak. "You're the only man I've ever baked anything for."

He was also the only man she'd ever lain chest-to-naked-chest with. A film of sweat formed on his forehead and he lost the struggle not to touch her again. He wanted her right now. "Don't be so sweet to me."

"Why shouldn't I?"

"Because I want my mouth on your breasts, my hands on your waist and my body so deeply buried in yours that I'll forget what we felt like apart."

She gasped softly. He didn't know what to make of her reaction until he found her stepping the slightest bit closer.

Swaying almost until her chest brushed against his. *Her nipples were hard.*

"I want to feel your curvy legs wrapped around my waist, your nails on my butt and your teeth on my shoulder. I'm not planning to stop until you're as wild for me as I am for you. But you've waited a long time to take a man into your body, Miranda, and it should be a different kind of man than I am."

She swayed again and he let go of her shoulders. The desire for her was so intense that if he kept touching her he'd lead off the road to a secluded little glen not twenty-five feet from the highway. A place where he'd be totally, completely alone with her.

That clear, crystal gaze met his and he grew hard. What his words had started, her eyes were finishing. She looked intrigued by the possibility that she made him react so intensely. He'd take her any way she came to him, even though he knew he wasn't what she needed.

He leaned down, resting his forehead against hers. Her breath brushed against his cheek, and he clenched his jaw against the need to pull her closer to him. He wanted to fit every soft curve of her body into every hard angle of his.

"Understand that this desire for you is more than an itch that can be scratched anywhere by anyone."

"Oh, Lord," she said, her voice anything but reverent.

In fact, Luke thought she sounded downright scared. "I'm not going to force you into sleeping with me."

"You wouldn't have to force me," she said softly, brushing her hand along his jaw. Luke felt her caring wrap around him like a living thing. In his soul the wild wind stopped howling for a moment.

"Luke, there is so much to me that you don't understand."

"It's crazy, isn't it? You're the complete opposite of every qualification I usually look for in women."

She smiled her sad sweet smile. "You like small-chested women?"

Her attempt at humor made his heart ache at not being the man she needed. "Ah, darlin'. The funny thing is, I like everything about you. And I don't see how we could make this work."

He forced her to step back, not able to stand the torment of being close but not close enough for one more minute.

She stood there staring at him as if he were some alien from another planet. "What now?"

"We have two choices—become lovers for the rest of the summer or stay the hell away from one another."

Miranda stared at him, making him feel big and mean, not for the first time, he recalled, but this time was infinitely worse because she should know him better by now.

"Let's take care of your car." Luke started for the Suburban. "Keep the wheel straight. I'll tow you to the service station."

"Luke—"

He stalked back to her, covering her mouth with his palm. "Not another word unless it's yes."

Miranda stood outside the repair shop for a long moment thinking about Luke's last statement. *Not another word unless it's yes.* God, the man loved ultimatums. But did she have the nerve to call him on it? She knew he wasn't playing a game with her. He'd reached the end of his restraint and the decision had to be up to her.

Focusing on the one thing she could really control, she pushed open the door to the garage. Miranda made arrangements with Mr. Hammings to have her car delivered to her town house in Atlanta once the repairs were made. The decision to return home hadn't been an easy one, but she couldn't stay and continue to torment Luke, even unintentionally, and she didn't want to tell him the truth—to see him look at her as if she were only half a woman.

The sound of thunder greeted her arrival back outside. A light but steady rain fell in a stream in front of her. She stared at the dark skies, wondering if luck would ever be on her side.

"What a day," she muttered. She loved a man for the first time in her life. The edgy, nervous feeling in the pit of her stomach wouldn't go away. All because a man— *Luke* desired her.

She paused on the stoop of the garage. How was she going to get back into town without getting wet?

"Miz Colby?"

Miranda faced Mr. Hammings. "Yes?"

"I have an old Jeep you can borrow."

"Thanks," she said. He handed her the keys and nodded toward the rust brown vehicle parked behind the pumps at the back of his property. The phone jangled inside the body shop and Mr. Hammings excused himself to go answer it.

She stared at the Jeep, wondering if she could actually drive something so…old, rusty, dirty. It wasn't that she was a snob. It was just that the vehicle looked as if it might bite. Her father had bought an old car for her and her sister to learn to drive on. She'd hated that car and the incompetent way she'd felt each time she'd gotten behind the wheel. But with determination and perseverance she'd learned to drive it.

"What's the matter, darlin'? Never driven a car older than yourself before?"

Why was he still here?

That voice sent a tingle down her spine and it pooled in the center of her body. She wrapped her arms protectively around her waist, weighing her next action very carefully. Glancing over her shoulder at him, she saw the tense set to his shoulders. Suddenly she knew she wasn't going to go back to Atlanta a virgin.

"Yes," she said.

His pupils expanded before his eyelids narrowed to slits.

Hands on his hips, he walked toward her with a carefully measured stride. He stopped when half the porch still stood between them.

"Yes, you've driven a car older than yourself?"

She pivoted to face him, edging slowly toward him. She shook her head.

"Darlin'!" he said, exasperation clear in his voice.

A gust of wind blew a wave of rain under the covering, soaking them both. He grabbed her wrist in a firm grasp and led her out to his truck.

Luke opened the door on the driver's side and Miranda wiped her sweating palms on her hips before climbing into the Suburban. She slid across the seat, not stopping until the passenger door was at her back.

Luke watched her intensely. Miranda shivered from sexual excitement. The daring of what she was about to do made her want to laugh hysterically.

The only sound to fill the cab was the pinging of raindrops against the roof. Miranda stared at Luke's face. All of her arguments and indecision seemed foolish now.

"Well?" he said. "What'd you mean out there?"

"I meant yes—to your earlier question."

"You're sure?"

"Yes."

"You'll become my lover?"

She nodded, fighting against the urge to throw herself into his arms, then decided to give in to the impulse. Luke caught her close, tightening his arms around her until she couldn't breathe. "Oh, darlin', you won't regret this."

Ten

Luke wanted to drive the truck off the road, find a secluded place to make love to Miranda—not a long, leisurely interlude; but a hot, frenzied coupling that would leave them both shaken and drained. Luke tempered the surge of lust and victory he felt at Miranda's surrender.

There were important things to be discussed and taken care of first. Things that weren't always easy for lovers to talk about. Things like birth control and medical history. Frankly, he'd never understood that attitude.

He wasn't stupid. The past had taught him a few important lessons that he'd never forget. The mistake of his first marriage still ruled in his mind. They'd married when she'd gotten pregnant—by his married brother he now knew.

He'd never wanted a woman the way he wanted Miranda and that made her dangerous. Normally, he had no problem controlling his body, controlling what he felt for the women he slept with, controlling his partners. Women who shared their body and passion but never their emotions. This lady was different.

She wasn't model slim or perfect, but she stirred to life the primal male inside him. The male who wanted to ravage and protect her. The male who needed to possess her completely.

Her mist gray eyes challenged him to stay honest. Her dark brown curls beckoned his fingers to tangle in the silky short length. Her sweet voice enticed him with every well-thought-out phrase she spoke.

Damn, but she pleased him on every level.

Her hand rested high on his thigh, her red nails looking sexy, tempting on the cloth of his dress pants. The long, slender fingers so close to his aching flesh made him harden in a rush. He shifted his legs, relieving little of the pressure.

He clenched his jaw. He wanted her. Even Suzanne hadn't affected him this intensely. *Suzanne*...and a baby that wasn't his.

"Are you on the Pill?" he asked gruffly.

The time for subtleties was gone. The reflex of the past came into play. Not the recent past, but automatic impulses left over from the beginning of time.

She'd surrendered to him. Now he sought to find the quickest means to quell the impatient desire that had been riding him since she'd arrived on his mountain looking lost, lonely and so heartbreakingly lovely that he hadn't stood a chance.

She glanced up sharply. The color drained from her face, leaving her normally healthy complexion washed-out and pale. Her fingers twitched nervously on his leg, nails digging almost painfully into his thigh. What the hell had he said to upset her?

"Darlin'?"

"No," she said softly. Her voice barely a decibel above the rain falling on the roof of the truck. "I've never taken the Pill."

She trembled as if afraid of being struck. Her voice too low and unemotional, almost as if he were inflicting a painful wound, which made no sense.

"When was your last medical examination?" he asked, hoping to God she'd had one recently.

She looked young and innocent, especially with her hair clinging to her scalp in wet ringlet curls. But looks were often deceiving.

"I don't have AIDS or any other sexually transmitted disease because I've never had sex. I give blood every three months at home and I'm an organ donor."

She fumbled to open her purse, and a minute later her driver's license and blood donor card were in his hands. "If you want to wait a few days, I can have my medical transcripts sent out."

Maybe he'd overreacted. But he'd rather err on the side of caution in this area of his life. He might not like living in a big town or city, but life still held enough promise to keep him hoping for several more years.

"That's not necessary," he said, reaching to cup her jaw. Her eyes were troubled as if she'd only realized the true implications of what she'd agreed to. "Second thoughts?"

She shrugged and tried to turn away.

"Tell me."

She closed her eyes as if not seeing him would make the words come easier. "Yes. I've never... I mean this is the first time I've started something like this."

"Want to change your mind?"

She shook her head, the mist in her eyes clearing. "Do you?"

"Hell, no."

"You're sure?" she asked, her gray gaze sparkling up at him. "I'm probably not going to be very good at this."

"Oh, darlin', yes, you are." She had no idea how much he wanted her.

"Were you a Boy Scout?"

"No, why?"

"You really believe in being prepared."

"I won't take chances with protection, darlin'. If that's a problem for you, let me know. But I want us completely protected from pregnancy."

"Okay. How were you burned?"

Miranda cared, he thought. The compassion she showed him strengthened the bond that lust had forged. "I told you about my marriage."

"I wouldn't manipulate you that way."

He saw the sheen of unshed tears in her eyes.

"That's a chance I won't take."

She turned away from him. He hated hurting her but lies would hurt more. He palmed his wallet from his back pocket and pulled out his donor card. "Just so you know, I give blood regularly."

She glanced at his card and handed it back. "I didn't think you'd have anything contagious," she said wryly.

"Why don't you take the Suburban home while I pick up some condoms?" he suggested.

"What are you going to drive?" she asked, still not looking at him.

"That hunk of junk Hammings tried to pawn off on you."

"I...thank you."

"You're welcome, darlin'."

He climbed out of the truck and into the rain-soaked afternoon. Leaning through the open door he kissed Miranda deeply. He didn't look back as he walked away, knowing that if he did, he would forget about protection, common sense and the past. Something he'd sworn never to do.

Miranda drove straight to her rented cabin, not paying attention to the steep road or the treacherous mud. Her mind dwelled on Luke's ex-wife, whom Miranda believed to be president of the Stupid Women Society. Even though she'd only known him for a short while, she knew that Luke demanded honesty from everyone around him.

Honesty. Something she hadn't given him completely. If only things were different, she thought.

The old rental cabin looked like home when she came around the bend. Her hands shook as she shut off the truck. Taking a deep, calming breath, she stepped out of the vehicle. The rainwater drenched her damp clothing.

Her mind fixed on the unbearable secret that she kept in the back of her mind. On one hand, that particular truth didn't matter to Luke. He wasn't planning to make a lifetime commitment to her. Though she wished it were otherwise, right now temporary was the only relationship she could maintain.

She changed into dry clothing before sitting on the unmade bed. What the heck was she thinking to agree to become Luke's lover? True, the man set her blood on fire, but there was so much more he needed to know before they made love. So much more that she really should tell him, now before she lowered her guard any farther. Once they made love certain things would be assumed. Lovers could ask questions that friends couldn't. She would have to face her past.

He would leave her.

She wouldn't blame him. She should stop this affair before it began. Her emotions told her it was too late. She already cared for Luke more than she should. "I'm no good at the games men and women play," she muttered.

She wasn't a femme fatale or glamour girl who drove men wild with lust. Yet Luke looked at her as if he'd never seen anyone lovelier. She'd endured lewd remarks and suggestive comments throughout adolescence, emerging into adulthood with a somewhat battered self-image.

Standing, she set the cabin to rights. The clean room mocked her with its quiet order, something her chaotic feelings couldn't attain. Miranda sighed. The wait strained her nerves to the breaking point.

She heard the hoarse chugging of the old engine as Mr. Hammings's battered truck made its way to her front yard. There was no doubt in Luke, Miranda realized.

He drove straight to her door and vaulted up the front steps. He paused on the other side of the screen looking at her with those dark brown eyes that could read the secrets in her soul. Eyes that bespoke of pleasure and a past filled with pain.

The chance to soothe that remembered hurt, to give a few days', weeks', months' respite to the self-enforced loneliness in Luke's life was one she couldn't pass up. She loved him and would enjoy whatever time fate deemed fitting for them. When the time came to tell him she couldn't have children she'd accept the end of their affair as naturally as she accepted the changes in Mother Nature, mourning the loss of spring and the long hot days of summer when the cold barren days of winter reigned.

Miranda reached for the door. It opened with a loud creaking that filled the silence on the porch. She dropped her hand from the frame as Luke stepped across the threshold. How had she doubted herself? She couldn't leave now. Her pulse sped up. She wanted this man more than anything she'd ever wanted—even a successful career.

Involuntarily she moved backward, allowing him only enough space to close the door. His heavy breathing betrayed his own nervousness which strangely reassured her.

Luke had experienced more of life's pleasures than she, but in this they were matched. This was the first time either of them had trusted another person.

Don't trust me, Luke.

Luke bent, his lips brushing against hers with a tenderness that made her heart ache. Never had a man cherished her, looking beyond the successful businesswoman. His tongue teased her lower lip, preparing it for the soft bite of his teeth. He tugged until her mouth opened under the passionate assault of his.

He tasted slightly salty and of the cigars that he smoked. A thirst unlike any she'd experienced welled up in her, a thirst to know all of him and to give him all of her. A thirst that would be sated before evening fell.

His work-roughened fingers traced the bones of her face, tilting her head back. His touch surprised her, reminding her of his strength. Miranda drank more of his essence from the kiss.

His hands swept down her back, grasping her hips and pulling her closer to his body. The hard length of his masculinity pressed urgently against her. She rocked her hips, enjoying the moan that came from the back of his throat. He felt so right pressed against her, that she rocked again.

Luke lifted his head, his eyes darker than ever before. Seeing her effect on him was a powerful aphrodisiac, and she wanted to wield that power. She wanted to increase his desire until he couldn't think of anything but her.

"Dammit, woman. You go to my head."

She ran her hands down his chest, caressing his hard pectoral muscles. Grasping his large hand with both of her smaller ones, Miranda led him across the room to the bed. The wrought iron frame and white linen sheets beckoned like a dream brought to life. Something so fantastic and unbelievable suddenly appearing in the flesh.

Finally, she thought. After years of waiting she'd know what all the excitement was about. Luke had brought her more than he could ever know or understand. He'd brought her a belief that she was a complete woman—not a "useless, empty shell masquerading as a female" as Warren had called her before ending their engagement.

His tanned arm reached past her, tossing back the coverlet. Then his hands fell heavily on her shoulders. He pulled her back against the lean strength of his chest. His warmth wrapped around her.

She felt the delicate bite of his teeth at her nape, then the wetness of his mouth. She trembled, feeling her breasts tighten and a heady warmth pool in her center. She leaned more fully into him.

His touch traveled downward, cupping her breasts. He stopped, teasing her with the anticipation. Currents of awareness radiated out from his stroking palms. Her nipples hardened in a rush. A long sigh escaped her lips.

"Like that?" he asked softly. His words caressing her neck as he spoke. He brushed his palm across her, rubbing as he waited for her response.

Tilting her head back, she glanced up at him. His features tightened by desire were fierce yet she didn't feel afraid. Miranda was glad that she was a woman at that moment. Glad that she was the woman here with Luke causing him to feel to the depths of his soul. Glad that she'd stood up to her fear.

"Oh, yes," she whispered, her voice sounding strange to her own ears.

"Good."

His deep drawling voice, lined with sincerity, reassured her. He pulled her shirt free of her shorts, sliding his hand up under her shirt. The slight trembling she felt in him reassured her. She wanted to be lying on the bed, face-to-face with him so she could explore him.

She stepped away from him and sat on the edge of the bed. He pushed her gently onto her back, positioning her on the bed. He tugged her shirt up over head and tossed it to the floor. Not giving her time to voice the protest she was forming, he took her bra away, too.

Her earlier exhilaration faded as she remembered her overblown form. She covered her breasts as she watched him remove his own shirt.

Pulling her hands away from her chest, he looked at her. She could only look at him—watch him watching her. The reverence in his gaze removed her inhibitions. She tugged her hands free of his grasp and let them settle at her sides.

He grinned a wicked tempting smile and she answered with one of her own. He came down on top of her, bracing his weight on his hands, pressing himself to her center. The pressure tantalizingly foreshadowed what was to come. Soon, she hoped.

"You are the sexiest woman I've ever met," he said in a raw, harsh voice. "I'm going to make you completely mine."

The heat of her blush should have set the bed on fire. His tongue traced a delicate design against her creamy flesh. His lips caressed the tips of her breasts and her doubts fled. His mouth engulfed her nipple, sucking strongly, tugging on her to receive succor.

She scored his chest with her fingernails, glorying in the way his breath sawed roughly in and out. The smooth pelt of dark curly hair invited her touch. She traced lightly over the differing textures of man, his smooth skin, silky hair and hardened nipples. She toyed with the narrow width of hair right above his waistband before sliding her index finger between cloth and skin. He groaned again, a deep sound that made her revel in her femininity.

She undid his belt and zipper, freeing his arousal from the confines of his dress pants and underwear. A reverent oath escaped his lips as she cupped the full masculinity in her grip. He was hot, hard and so tempting. Her grip slid lower, holding the softest flesh on his body in her palm.

"Darlin'. You're killing me."

He quickly stripped her shorts and panties down her legs. Standing, he rid himself of the rest of his clothing. He stared at her and she felt pride in herself. She spread her arms and legs, allowing him to see all of her.

He walked across the floor, muscles alternately bunching and relaxing. He walked like a cowboy, she thought wryly. He retrieved the package he'd dropped at the door.

Condoms.

He returned to the bed to lay on his side, propped on his elbow. His free hand swept down her body, parting the moist delta at the apex of her thighs. His questing touch readied her for his possession. When he inserted one finger into her, she couldn't control her hips, surging upward to take more of him.

Heaven knew she wanted this man as she'd wanted no other. If he didn't take her soon, she'd die.

Every nerve in her body rushed toward something, and she had a feeling that she was going to experience her first orgasm before he even entered her. He moved his fingers again; the movement made her tense. She wanted more.

She stroked his arousal once more, bringing a drop of his essence from him. She shuddered with him. He cursed rawly and she knew that he'd reached the edge of his control. It was one of the most emotional things she'd ever experienced. She no longer doubted her attractiveness or even that she was a passing fancy to this man.

"I've been wanting you for so long."

He looked at her as if he were searching for the solution to life's problems. He looked at her as if she were his salvation and his temptation in one package.

She wanted to feel the entire length of his body pressed against hers. She needed him. *Now.*

"I've never been a woman's first lover before," he said haltingly.

He took a condom from the box and ripped the package open.

"Let me."

He bent and bit her nape. "I wish I could, darlin'. But I wouldn't last."

Condom in place, he returned to kiss her again. He slid slowly into her body, allowing her time to adjust to his penetration. He was a big man, she thought as he stroked deeper inside of her.

He eased his hand between their bodies and stroked the tiny nubbin hidden in her nest of curls. Finally the relentless nerves that had been surging toward something found their release, and she shook with the force of her climax, barely aware that he slid past the barrier of her virginity.

He held her while the tremors rocked her body. When she was still at last, he began a strong rhythm that renewed her tingle from head to toe. She held him in a grip that wouldn't lessen as he pumped into her body, and when he found his own climax, she felt like a complete woman.

Here was a man she'd love for a lifetime. A one-of-a-kind man meant only for her, and he wouldn't stay that long. Unbidden tears welled up and slid slowly down her cheeks.

Oh, damn, what had she done?

Luke had long since decided that the events that cost the most were in the long run those that felt the best. After tonight's work, he figured that he'd signed the papers closing the deal for his eternity in hell. Yet he couldn't regret taking Miranda's virginity.

Miranda's sweet innocence had soothed some long-forgotten wound. Something so deep and so painful that he'd hidden it even from himself. He reached for the coverlet, pulling it over the both of them.

She sighed and snuggled deeper into him, as if she could absorb his body into hers by touch alone. He wished it were so. There was something so alive in the feel of her pressed close to him.

Despite the fact that she had run to these woods to hide from her past, she hadn't hidden the way he had. She still embraced life, she was still willing to live it and find the good. She still cared for people and things. She still believed in happily ever after, he realized abruptly.

Oh, hell.

He couldn't offer her what she most deserved. He

couldn't even ask her to accept less because doing so would ruin what they had. He figured he'd lucked out when she'd interrupted his bath that day. Or maybe fate had a hand in it, because he rarely bathed in the outdoor tub. He'd used it primarily when he'd been building his house.

Now they were engaged in an affair. Passion still burned too brightly to blow this off as a one-night stand. Miranda didn't go in for casual sex and neither did he any longer.

She sighed and mumbled something in her sleep. He pulled her snugly against his chest, cradling her. The bounty of her breasts pressed against him. He leaned down, dropping a kiss on the top of her head.

She rubbed her cheek against his chest in response. Miranda reacted wonderfully to his every touch. As if she were made only to be his lover. As if no other man could make her reach the heights of her own pleasure and the depths of her own emotions. As if she'd been waiting her entire life for him.

This quiet sharing time after passion was new to him. Luke had never wanted to linger before. Never needed to share the hugs and soft kisses in the moonlight.

The light from the moon spilled in through the open curtains. The rain had stopped and the clouds cleared away, leaving behind only the stars. Luke wished they were at his place. The windows surrounding the loft left a great view of the night. He knew Miranda would enjoy seeing it.

Her relaxation was complete as she lay in his arms. He doubted she'd slept any better than he had these past few days. The knife edge of passion was now dulled temporarily.

He stared down at her dark hair. The silky stuff felt like a kitten's fur against his chest. He'd never felt anything so…*right*.

And it scared him.

Passion he understood and could handle, but the emotional side of life had a way of backfiring. Luke couldn't sleep that night. He watched the soft stages of dawn slowly creep into the room, leaving it drenched in sunlight. He carefully untangled himself from Miranda.

She'd wrapped herself around him while she slept and he'd never felt anything half as good. Outside of sex with her, he amended.

The sun streaked through the open curtains, painting Miranda's skin in a dappled hue. She sighed and stretched, and the sheet slipped down her back stopping at the curve of her waist.

Luke stood where he was across the cabin. His first instinct had been to leave before she woke. But he couldn't do that to her. It would be too much like abandoning her. He didn't want to leave her until she was out of his system. Until he stopped getting hard every time he looked at her.

She stirred and wakened. "Luke?"

"Here, darlin'."

Her mist gray eyes met his and he realized that he wanted to spend the rest of the summer with her. He wanted her to live in his house, eat in his kitchen and sleep in his bed.

Filling one of the chipped mugs with coffee, he carried it to her. She held the sheet to her chest with one hand and reached for the mug with the other. He sat down next to her without releasing the steaming cup.

Leaning back against the wrought iron headboard, he set the coffee on the nightstand. "Scoot back here against me."

She shook her head.

"Why not?"

She covered her mouth with her hand. "I have morning breath."

Luke studied her carefully. Obviously this was important to her. He lifted the mug to his lips and took a large sip, but didn't swallow it all. He gently wrapped his hand around the back of her neck and brought her face close to his. He kissed her, letting the coffee seep from his mouth into hers. At first, she was stiff and unyielding but then she relaxed, taking from his mouth the warm liquid.

He lifted his head reluctantly, and smiled at her. "Not anymore."

She slid back until she rested against him. He wrapped his arms around her torso, enjoying the warm, sensual feel of this woman in the morning. *His woman.*

He nuzzled the side of her neck, thinking that everything would be just about perfect if...

"Will you move in with me?"

Eleven

Will you move in with me?

The words echoed through her mind like a gavel in an empty courtroom. Her hands shook and a block of ice took up residence in her stomach. The panic attack sent chills spreading outward to each limb, freezing the blood in her veins.

"What did you say?" she asked in a squeaking tone. No other word accurately described the sound her voice made.

She scooted sideways, facing him. His expression bore no signs of confusion. Where had this come from? It was so sudden. "I didn't understand you."

She tucked the sheets under her armpits before wrapping her arms around her waist. Last night was…one moment out of time, she thought. She should have told him before they'd made love that she was only half a woman. Now he thought…

"I'm not talking about forever—neither of us wants that. But this ragged old cabin isn't the best place to live and my place is nice. *Really nice.* And the way I feel about you right now—well, dammit, Miranda, I want you with me.''

"Oh." Unexpected tears stung her eyes. She appreciated his honesty. She couldn't believe her luck in finding a man like Luke. A man who faced the future the same way she'd always tried to—with her eyes open. Something Warren never had. He had had his own vision for the future and never shared with her his feelings about their life together. With Luke she knew where she stood.

Yet, at the same time he cared about her. *What a sweet man.* Feeling infinitely precious to him, she slid closer, not stopping until she could touch him and feel his hot skin beneath her fingers. He wrapped her in a big bear hug, resting his head on top of hers.

The long strands of his dark hair brushed against her cheek. She rubbed her face against his soft locks, enjoying the feeling. Luke offered her so much. This was the chance of a lifetime. She'd already decided to have a summer affair with him.

"Don't run scared on me now. I just want a chance to see if we like each other under normal circumstances."

"Normal?" Living in the woods would never seem normal to her. A quick glance at his expression confirmed that he already knew that. This cohabitation would be temporary, like their affair. It would last until one of them wised up and moved on. A bittersweet feeling engulfed her, leaving her trembling in its wake. To not take this chance would be like cutting off her arm. To take it would be like... embracing sunlight.

She believed Luke didn't want anything permanent in his life on the off chance that it might make him care again. She regretted the bitterness of her thoughts even as they coalesced in her mind. She carefully smothered the thought.

She had a choice to make. She could turn him down and watch him leave now. Or...she could live with him throughout the summer, storing up the memories for when they were no longer together.

"Darlin', don't make so much of my offer. Do you want to live with me for the summer, spending the days learning outdoor lore and the evenings up in the loft? The bank of glass windows makes you feel like you can touch the stars and, of course, you'll probably feel like I'm taking you there."

She smiled at the lack of modesty in his voice. Luke had a right to the assurance he felt at his ability to please a woman. He'd certainly made her come alive in a way no other man ever had.

"I can't," she said regretfully. Honesty demanded that she be forthright with him and she didn't want to lose him yet. She'd only just discovered what it felt like to be loved, to be cared for. She wouldn't give that up yet.

"Why not?"

He slid his callused palm under her chin, lifting her face to his. Watching her with a seemingly limitless well of patience.

She bit her lower lip. Not normally indecisive, she blurted out the truth before she could screen the words. "I don't think I'd like living with a man."

"That's a sweeping statement, Miranda. I'm not just any man."

"I know that," she said, tears clogging her throat. She caressed his cheek with her hand and watched his eyes narrow. He started to speak but she covered his mouth with her fingers.

"Believe me, I'll disappoint you."

He gently moved her fingers from his lips. "Like you disappointed me in bed?"

She felt her face heat up, and forced herself to keep looking him in the eye. Every instinct screamed for her to hide, to avoid having this conversation, but she couldn't.

"Let me be the judge of what disappoints me. And I'm not your ex-fiancé."

"Oh, Luke," she said, softening. "I'm not cut out for the daily ins and outs that men expect."

His wicked laughter made her realize what she'd just said. Her face felt as if she'd been burned by the sun. She slapped his shoulder lightly. "I didn't mean that."

"Damn, darlin'. That's the one thing I can help you adjust to," he said between chuckles. The humor left his expression. "Just give it a try. Stay with me for the rest of the week."

No, her rational mind said. Don't do it. The crazy side of her nature taunted her with images of her and Luke as they'd been last night.

Sunlight, after years of darkness.

She opened her mouth to say no, but nodded instead. For once, she was going to choose a path she'd never traveled before. A path that might lead her to the greatest gift life has to offer—love—or a path that might lead to heartbreak. But she'd been down that one before. She'd guard against disappointment, living for the moment.

His mouth took hers in a savage kiss that left her feeling as if she'd been marked as his for eternity.

The summer breeze blew through the open door, stirring the hair at the back of Luke's neck. The room was dark. He preferred it that way, using only a single light to relieve the utter blackness. No windows to distract him from his work, no extra lights to blur the vision he used as his guide. His attention to the block of wood in front of him never wavered. He'd escaped the house to give Miranda time to settle in and to give himself time to adjust to her presence.

He'd wanted to emit a yell when she'd stepped over the threshold with her belongings, but hadn't. Acknowledging the primal man inside was dangerous for him. Luke preferred to ignore that instinctive beast for as long as possible.

The large piece of balsam had finally revealed its secrets. Luke closed his eyes, locking the vision firmly in place before beginning to work on a rocking chair. He hummed a country-western tune under his breath absently.

He shed his shirt as the temperature in the shop began to rise. Ignoring the splintering wood chips that fell on his chest, he used the knife to detail the back of the chair.

A sound at the door caught his attention. Sensing no danger, Luke froze nonetheless. Nature seemed still and quiet in that instant, as if paused for a specific reason.

His world shifted. Miranda cleared her throat softly, though he knew instinctively that it was her. He didn't have friends or neighbors who dropped by unexpectedly.

The breeze stirred again, this time carrying a distinctive scent. The smell of her skin and perfume etched firmly into his sensory banks. He breathed deeply, filtering out the fragrance of the wood until only her distinctive essence remained.

Her gaze touched his back like a living flame, tracing over the tattoo on his shoulder. He tensed as the fire of arousal licked slowly through his veins pooling between his legs. The muscles of his upper back flexed in response.

He pivoted slowly to face her. Miranda stood in the doorway framed by sunlight, her face in shadow. The hesitant posture told him that she was as unfamiliar as he with this situation. It would be different if they lived together in the city where she'd have her job and friends, but on the side of his mountain they were completely alone.

He should invite her in. Welcome her to his workshop but he didn't want to. Honesty demanded that he admit he was afraid to let her in.

Miranda stepped carefully out of the sunlight to join him in the dark cavern of his shop. He yanked the protective goggles off his head, tossing them in the direction of the worktable that held his tools. The action knocked the bare bulb of the light above his head. It swung, making a creaking sound that filled the silent workroom.

He set his knife down. Miranda stopped behind him, her breath brushing against his back, her fingers resting lightly on his arm.

"I'm finished in the house. I'm looking forward to washing in your garden tub and shower upstairs. I was afraid you'd insist on bathing outside every day."

The thought of her naked in the tub on his back porch triggered an avalanche of need. He wanted a fierce joining of their bodies, a surcease to the tension that pervaded his body. "Give me a minute to finish up in here and we'll go find something to do."

"I don't want to disturb you."

"Hell, darlin', just picturing you in my house 'disturbed' me." And she did. He pictured her on his bed in the loft clothed in nothing but a sheen of sweat.

"How?" As always her innocent questions kept him on edge. How could the woman who made his blood boil hotter than the fires of hell have no idea of her own appeal?

"One guess." The guttural tone of his voice bothering him.

Her fingers moved then, tracing over the design on his shoulder, her touch soft as the predawn mists that ringed the mountain. Fighting the urge to touch her, he clenched his fists.

"Did you draw this?" she asked, changing the subject. He knew that any type of sexual innuendo or teasing bothered her.

"The design?" he countered, drawing out an inane conversation.

"Mmm-hmm," she murmured against his skin. Her tongue following the trail her fingers had taken.

"Why did you pick a hawk?"

Her teasing touch inflamed him and he could hardly

string two coherent words together. *The hawk*... "I wanted to remind myself of who I am."

"Who are you?"

"A predator."

She touched her mouth to his skin again and he couldn't take it another moment.

"Miranda," he said harshly as he lost the battle with his self-control.

"You don't have to stop to entertain me." Her lips moved against his skin as she spoke.

"What are you going to do?" he asked, to make sure that she was aware that this type of play could end in only one way.

"Watch you."

If she didn't stop touching him... He stepped away breaking her contact with him. He faced her, watching the disappointment in her expression, but didn't say anything or try to keep him close. Any other time it would have bothered him, but right now her reaction fit his mood.

"Let's get out of here before I lose what little common sense I still have."

"What's that mean?"

Miranda had to categorize every statement and emotion. He figured it came from her dealing with numbers more than she dealt with people. "Only that I don't want to be attacking you every second of the day."

"Attacking?"

"*Seducing* would be a better word."

"Oh, sex."

The way she dismissed sex as having any importance in her life annoyed him. Maybe it was a guy thing, but dammit all, she should treat the powerful attraction between them with a little more respect. "Not sex, making love."

"Semantics," she said softly.

"Not semantics unless you think this is a casual thing.

Unless last night was the only time you'll let me inside you."

She shivered at his words. "I'm still new to this."

"Hell, darlin', so am I. Never has one woman affected me the way you do."

"Me, too," she said quietly again. "I think I'll go back to the house and try my hand at baking. I really didn't mean to intrude on your work. I just..."

"What?" he asked, feeling raw from explaining his feelings for her, needing her to be as naked as he.

"I missed you."

He couldn't stay away from her. He needed to touch, to consume, to possess her. He needed to be home again, inside her, feeling her wrapped all around him, silky, hot...

"Come on," he said, lifting her roughly into his arms.

She started to speak but he stopped her words with a harsh kiss that came from deep inside him. He knew that it was a mistake to let her affect his life this way, but also realized it was too late to stop her influence. A strange feeling not unlike light-headedness streaked through him as he acknowledged the source of her power over him.

He could love her.

Miranda stood in front of the mirror, staring at the red silk dress. The fabric lovingly caressed every curve of her full-bodied figure. It was the kind of dress she'd always avoided buying because it revealed too much of her, clinging to every hollow. But Luke had gone shopping with her and his eyes had glazed over when he'd looked at it on the rack.

She sighed, knowing it was dangerous to let one man have that much control over her emotions. But she wouldn't regret it. She was happier now than she'd been in her entire life. She didn't even miss her job anymore.

A wolf whistle pierced the silence of the room. She glanced up as Luke walked into the room, stopping behind her. He rested his hands on her shoulders. His eyes met hers in the mirror. Her blood pounded fiercely through her veins, warming her to the core. In the three weeks since they'd become lovers, she should have gotten used to his touch, but she hadn't.

Luke had signed a big contract with a nearby resort to provide all the carpentry. Miranda was taking him out to dinner in Jessup Springs to its one nice restaurant to celebrate.

His touch was still new—fresh and exciting. The dress pants and string tie fit him perfectly. Everyday clothes enhanced his masculinity, but the dress clothes made him seem sexier than ever.

He looked more like a cover model in his Armani dress suit than her quiet mountain man, his long hair once again tied at the back of his neck with a leather thong. The diamond stud earring glittered wickedly in the glow of the lamplight.

"Oh, Luke. You're devastating."

He grinned slyly at her and winked. "We aim to please."

"I'm going to be fighting the women off you all evening."

"I'll depend on you to defend my virtue, darlin'."

The brilliant color of her dress stood out against the stark black and white of his clothing, like a colorful shadow pressed against him. The softness of the cloth of his suit pressed against her back. Her skin tingled from the contact.

He traced a line down the center of her back. His callused fingers sending wonderful shivers outward from each stroke. She tried to step away from his caress but bumped into the vanity.

"Where are you going, darlin'?" he asked, his voice so low and rough that the words were barely discernible.

"Nowhere. We have to leave in a few minutes."

"I know," he said, his tone regretful.

He kissed the point where her neck met her collarbone.

Sucking briefly—too briefly, then biting gently. Leaving his mark on her skin and heart once again.

"I have a gift for you."

She tried to quell the excitement running rampantly through her. Not from the mention of a gift but from his intimate touch. A touch that her body had been accustomed to having when it wanted. A touch she wanted much more of.

"What is it?" Her voice, husky from need, shocked her.

Luke grinned in a way that made him look like the devil's first lieutenant before reaching into his breast pocket. He pulled out a small velvet box. For a moment fear shot through her heart, disrupting the beautiful feelings of only a second earlier. But she quickly reminded herself that marriage was a mistake that Luke would never make again.

They'd had many intimate discussions over the past few days. Enough for her to know that Luke Romero wasn't going to risk his emotional security on a man-woman relationship.

"Close your eyes."

She followed his direction.

His breath stirred the hair at her nape. She tensed, feeling extremely vulnerable to him. His fingers slid around her neck, then were replaced by a feather-light touch.

"Okay, darlin'."

She peeked through the veil of her lashes, meeting his brown gaze in the mirror. His fingers on her neck drew her eyes there. She followed the trail of a thin gold chain to the pendant that lay nestled right above the voluptuous curves of her cleavage.

The small heart-shaped diamond made tears choke her throat. Never before had she been gifted with anything half as lovely. Never before had she felt a man had come into her very soul and taken up residence. Never before had she loved so completely that to lose Luke would mean losing a vital part of her own self.

Without design, the tears started to fall. She bit her lip, trying to hid her emotional reaction. But Luke watched in the mirror. He turned her into his embrace, tucking her cheek against his chest, rubbing his big hands down her back as he attempted to comfort her.

The gentle touch evoked more tears. Though he wasn't mean, Luke *was not* a gentle man. She couldn't stop crying and feeling. Oh, God, she never should have come here— lived here with this man.

He forced her head upward and bent to take her mouth in a savage kiss. His tongue penetrated her mouth deeply, leaving no part unexplored. Her breathing altered, her nipples hardened and her pulse accelerated.

The tears choking her disappeared. She clung to Luke as if he were her lifeline. And perhaps he was. His lips left hers to sip the tears from her cheeks. Touched deeply by the gesture, she lifted her palms to his face.

"Thank you."

"You okay?"

"Yes. No one's ever given me..."

He dropped a soft kiss on her brow and hugged her close. "I'm glad."

She absorbed the solidness of his body wrapped around hers into her memory banks, squeezing him tightly before letting go. "I bet I look a mess."

"You're lovely, as usual."

She returned to the vanity to repair her makeup. Luke lounged on the unmade bed. Miranda felt a homey, husband-and-wife sense of well-being and felt as if time were running out. Each day they grew closer and closer, and she knew that she had to tell him the truth about herself—soon. She turned to him. "Well?"

He walked over to her, grasping her wrists and holding

her arms out from her sides. Then, releasing her left hand, he spun her around slowly.

"Breathtaking," he said against her neck, nibbling his way down the length of her new gold necklace. He lifted the charm and laved the spot where it had rested with his tongue. He dropped the charm and stood. "To remind you of me when we're apart."

She followed him out of the bedroom, glimpsed over her shoulder at the bedroom as they left. The sight of their possessions intertwined on the bed made her hope.... *Things might work out after all.*

Twelve

After dinner Luke suggested stopping at a nearby resort for drinks and dancing. Miranda wanted his arms around her while they listened to the slow bluesy music.

She watched Luke while he stood at the bar looking big, bold and primitive. She shivered with joy as she realized once again he was her man.

She'd surrendered not only to demands that she live with him, but also to the warmth of his passion.

He returned to their table with two glasses of wine and she watched the other women in the bar as they studied Luke. Jealousy lanced through her. He might be her man now, but how long could it last? How long before he realized that something was missing in their lives? How long before he asked her for more than she could give? How long before he walked away from her, never to return?

He set the drinks on the table. Imperiously, he held his hand out to her as if he were the emperor and she his favorite concubine. Her pulse rate increased and her breathing became shallow. Sophistication was highly over-rated, she thought. She'd take raw sexuality and passion any day. Not yet. If she gave in too easily, he'd think he had her tamed, and she wanted to continue to challenge him.

She arched one eyebrow and gave him the cold perilous look that came from years as an executive. She shook her head.

He sighed.

She heard the sound over the din of voices in the room. She fought the urge to laugh at his disgruntled expression. Grinning in the sexy teasing way he'd taught her, she crooked her finger at him.

He leaned in, his aftershave reminding her of their early-morning lovemaking in the steamy shower. She wanted him again.

Trembling now with desire and frustration, she stood.

"Darlin'."

Luke's voice started a chain reaction in her soul like the death of a supernova spreading energy through the universe. The shivers radiated out from her center, leaving her skin aching for his touch.

Luke's hard, callused palm rested on her back, just below the daring vee in the back of her dress as he led her to the dance floor. The sprawl of his fingers permitted his forefinger access to her skin. He stroked the small area, seemingly without notice.

The crowd around them slowly disappeared and Miranda faced him. His breath brushed the hair at her temple and his eyes held hers.

Miranda's breasts felt heavy and a familiar warmth pooled in the center of her body. Luke didn't say another word to her. Suddenly she'd had enough of this teasing. *She wanted him.* At the very least she'd settle for his arms wrapped around her.

Taking a leaf from Luke's book, she led him through the

crowd farther onto the floor. The jazz combo play
melancholy strains of Duke Ellington's "Sophisti d
Lady." For once she felt like the lady in the song. Classy,
cultured, capable of anything.

She put her arms around his neck and cuddled closer.
Luke's hands spanned her waist as he moved slowly to the
music. The brushing of his hardened body against her lower
stomach made her feel alive in a way she only felt in his
arms.

She relaxed for the first time all evening. All her life
she'd driven toward the goal of social standing, monetary
gain and a top-level executive position with lots of fringe
benefits. Suddenly those goals paled in comparison with
Luke. A lifetime of ideals couldn't compete with Luke and
the solace she found in his arms and with his company.

Dangerous line of thinking.

A need for Luke's presence in every corner of her life
warned that her secrets needed to be shared before she
started to care deeply for him. Too late, she thought. Already she loved him, and though trusting a man was something she'd never feel entirely comfortable with, she had to
tell him the truth about herself.

Continued silence would hurt him. She decided that tonight she'd tell him. Tell him that she'd never really make
any man happy, tell him that part of her would always fear
a man's control in her life, tell him that she could *never*
have a child.

"Enjoying yourself?" he asked, his husky voice caressing her.

"Yes," she said. Nothing could bother her when she was
with Luke like this—pressed gently against him and
wrapped in the security of his presence. She forgot her
worries and fears that he'd leave her if he ever knew her
secret. She forgot that she was a barren shell of a woman.
She forgot everything but the joy of being with Luke.

"I'm not," he muttered.

"Not enjoying the dancing?" she asked, trying to sound light and teasing, but feeling a heavy weight settle in her stomach at the thought of what she must tell him tonight.

He laughed and squeezed her tight against him, running one of his hands down her bare back. "Holding a tempting bundle like you will always be enjoyable. It's this damned suit. I wish I'd worn jeans and a T-shirt."

"Me, too." Miranda played with the hair at the back of his neck. Twirling the length around her finger before she released it. God, he was sexy.

"You like the way I look in jeans?"

"Umm-hmm, especially those indecent ones you wear around the house. They cling to your butt and they're so faded that I'm sure if you bend they'll rip." She moved her fingers to his neck and caressed the tendons there. She felt his pulse quicken beneath her fingers and glanced up at him. His brown eyes were as dark and compelling. Her breath caught and she licked her lips, leaning forward...wanting to tempt him into a kiss.

"I had no idea you were eyeing me that way."

She had no idea what he was talking about. She only knew that she wanted...no, needed to feel closer to him. To feel as if she was a part of him and his life. To feel his mouth on hers making her forget so much of the past.

"Eyeing you?"

He kissed her gently on her brow, her cheek and finally her lips. "Darlin', are you listening to me?"

"I'm trying, but the music is soothing and your voice makes me want to curl up against you."

She sounded disgruntled to her own ears. Leaning up she kissed him. Thrusting her tongue past the barrier of his teeth, she tasted *him*—her man. Luke took over then. Tilting his head, he conquered her, maybe as retribution for her earlier teasing. She didn't know, didn't really care. The deep passionate embrace left her trembling and him breathing heavy.

He held her close for the remainder of the song and Miranda savored the embrace. Her secret still loomed in her subconscious like a nightmare monster under a child's bed. For the moment she pushed it out of view until the lights were shut off again and she was cast back into the dark alone.

The night sky glittered with stars and a full moon. Luke paid scant attention to nature's beautiful display, thinking once again of Miranda.

Miranda snored softly in the passenger seat of the Suburban. He drew deeply on his cigar as he drove home. Taking more care than he normally did by lowering his speed almost to the limit for once.

He was changing. In the past, he'd always fought change and lost. But with Miranda his thinking was colored. Something was very different about her and her influence on his life.

Why would she settle for an open-ended relationship with a battered ex-rodeo rider?

He stubbed the cigar out. It wasn't having its usual soothing effect on his nerves. Perhaps because he didn't really know what he wanted. The brief hope he'd entertained of changing disappeared. He couldn't live in the city. Even Jessup Springs got on his nerves if he stayed in town too long. He needed the open air and trees. He needed the soft, gray mists so like Miranda's eyes because they soothed the savage part of him. *Soothed and comforted.* The only other time he'd even come close to that feeling was in Miranda's arms.

Not during their lovemaking, but afterward, when the night was alive with sound, the stars and moon twinkled down on them through the glass windows, and her heart beat steadily against his chest. Only then he could relax and not have to feel unguarded.

She'd given him a gift he'd never realized he'd wanted.

She'd given him a way to come to terms with the man he was and the ideal his family had always wanted. He'd bet his cabin on the fact she'd had no idea what she was doing.

She stirred when they arrived at the cabin but didn't waken until he'd carried her inside. He needed some answers from her and though she was sleepy he planned to get them tonight.

"Are we home?" she asked, her drowsy voice more than a little arousing.

Home. The word had many different meanings and he'd never applied it to any place but his family's ranch. He never thought it could be more than a place. Now he realized home could mean anything, a feeling or a person. "Yeah, darlin', we are."

"Good. I liked going into the city but I'm glad to be back here. The mountains are...soothing."

He smiled. Her voice filled with the wonder that new knowledge often brings. She was a tempting bundle and her body relaxed against his. He crossed to the couch and set her carefully on it.

"Want some coffee?" he asked, unsure how to proceed with his questioning. He didn't want her to feel like she was on the witness stand and he was a lawyer demanding to know every intimate detail of her life. But there were some things he needed to hear from her.

"Yes, please."

He started a fire in the fireplace before going to fix the coffee. The entire time he waited for the pot to brew he cautioned himself to take things slow and easy. To act like the kind, caring, civilized man that Miranda deserved.

By the time the coffee was ready he felt as though he was about to explode.

He grabbed two mugs, sloshed the hot brown liquid into them and stalked down the hall to the living room.

Luke froze as his gaze encountered Miranda sitting on the couch. The firelight played across her creamy skin, highlighting the slightly rounded planes of her face. She had her eyes closed and her cheek turned to the fire. The red dress hugged every curve of her body as she reclined against the cushions.

The rhythm of her breathing caused her breasts to come tantalizingly close to escaping the flimsy confines of her bodice. He imagined himself, brushing the straps of her dress off her shoulders, touching her soft skin, bringing her nipples to readiness with his fingers. Then suckling and drawing from her the essence only she could provide.

"Miranda."

She opened her eyes but didn't sit up. "I'm glad you're back. I missed your arms around me."

Her words touched a hidden scarred part of his soul.

"I need to know something," he said, trying to be gentlemanly.

"What?"

"Miranda, why…" Oh, hell, he couldn't be subtle. He wasn't built for it. He was a big, bold man and he lived his life that way.

"Why the hell are you living with me?"

Why the hell are you living with me?

The words echoed in her head like the maniacal laughter of a crazed jester, circling round and round. She cringed, wanting to cover her ears but sat stock-still. The need to demand he repeat the question was almost more than she could bear. Biting her lip, she kept the words from escaping.

Breathe deeply, she cautioned herself. Lifting her head, she met his unflinching gaze. Gone was the passionate lover who'd held her in his arms. The sheer eroticism that had marked each of his movements was banked, and in its place was an unbreakable determination for something. She had no idea what he really wanted from her. More than sex, she realized suddenly. More than the caring that she'd given him with the hope that he'd someday return it. More than…she was capable of giving to him.

Slowly she regained control over her jumbled senses. "I…I don't know what you want from me."

"I want the truth, darlin'. Why would a woman with your assets settle for a temporary relationship…"

With me.

Miranda heard the words even though he didn't say them out loud. Her arms ached with the need to wrap him in a hug and soothe away the wounds revealed by that level question. His doubts in himself reassured her in a way that she'd never felt before. That this man, this sexy, confident, sure-of-himself man, had doubts about himself and their relationship made her feel almost giddy, yet at the same time scared.

Oh, God, she thought suddenly, don't let me hurt him any more than he already has been.

She knew then that her love for him wouldn't be a smooth, tranquil emotion that would soothe her, but a turbulent, chaotic feeling that would always keep her unsteady. Curses rose in the back of her throat and she was afraid to open her mouth lest they escape. How was she going to find the courage to tell him she couldn't have kids?

The truth. In essence a principle that she believed in but at this moment she hid from. Wanting to hedge, knowing she couldn't, she opened her mouth but the words wouldn't come. She didn't want to see disappointment in his eyes. Didn't want to hear the excuses he'd make before leaving her. Didn't want to face the mountain morning without him by her side.

I can't have kids. "I'm not sure how to answer your questions."

"It's not just sex, Miranda. You need more. I don't feel capable of giving you more."

"Well, that's to the point. We've got to do something about your verbal skills."

"Dammit, darlin', you know I'm not civilized most of the time. I'm rough around the edges and I don't know how to change the way I am. Frankly I don't think I want to."

"Luke, don't worry about verbal skills. You have no problems with communication. I like that you're blunt."

"*You're not.*"

She nodded, she'd learned long ago how to cover bad news with good. How to hedge and edge and talk without revealing an honest emotion. She wished now that she hadn't. In some ways she was more experienced than Luke.

She wanted—no, needed—to change the subject. "You looked very sophisticated in your suit."

He gave her one of those looks that said he thought she was insane. She just grinned as she walked over to him. Reaching up she loosened his tie, toying with the metal tips at the ends of the string.

"How do I look?"

He smiled indulgently before winking at her. Tracing her nose and jaw with one finger, he leaned in and brushed his lips over the plane of her cheeks. The soft, warm touch of his mouth on her skin made shivers of awareness course through her body.

"Gorgeous, sophisticated, charming. Like a woman who could have anything in the world she wanted. Which leads me back to my original question. Why would you live with me when you could have everything a woman would want?"

She had no idea how he defined the needs of every woman. He had everything she'd ever wanted in a man and more. No, that wasn't true. Her ideal had been a cardboard cutout of the "perfect" man. Some image that couldn't be fulfilled by any human.

Luke was so much more. He had a lusty way of looking at life that she'd never experienced before. Despite his dark

side, he was still a very outgoing, live-life-on-the-edge type
of person.

"What would *every woman* want?" she demanded,
needing to understand his insecurities.

"A man who can provide her with security. A man she
can marry and raise kids with...a man who's not like me."

She didn't believe he thought she wanted those things.
She did want them but they would never be hers. She realized then that pain was the only end to this evening.
Which was a shame because she'd actually begun to feel
cared for, maybe even loved.

"Oh, Luke." She didn't know what to say to him, but
she felt he'd just bared his soul to her. Revealed things that
were hard for him to say out loud. God, this was hard. She
hadn't wanted to be able to hurt him, and she just realized
that she had the power to.

"I want you to know up-front that I'll never offer you
marriage. I'll never father a child, either, because I can't
go through loving and losing another child. But, lady,
you've shown me that trusting a woman doesn't have to be
a dangerous thing."

Oh, God. He's never going to be able to trust me again.
"Luke, there are reasons why my engagement ended. Reasons why I'd never slept with a man before you walked
into my life. Reasons I never shared with you before because..."

She hesitated wanting to be honest but not wanting to be
vulnerable. Luke stared at her as she sat down, his eyes
deep with caring. She felt him silently urging her on.

"I was afraid to tell you. I still am."

"Don't be afraid, darlin'. I'd never hurt you."

Physically, she'd never been safer, but emotionally...
never before had a man meant so much to her on so many
different levels. She shook with fear every time she thought
of life without him. Part of her *knew* that he'd leave

once she told him. Warren had called her cold, callous and uncaring, and she agreed with him.

"There are things about me that will make me less than desirable to you once you know them. Things that you probably never thought I'd keep from you and I know now that I shouldn't have.

"But, it was so nice to have a man like you look at me like I was a whole woman. Like I was someone worthy of that desire, and so I just kept quiet and hoped you wouldn't notice."

"What didn't you tell me?" he asked. His voice became deathly silent as he walked to the fireplace. The logs crackled, filling the room with that eerie sound.

She rose to her feet, needing to feel a little less like the subservient woman. "I…"

"Spit it out, dammit." The anger in him palpable. She'd betrayed him. Had gone into things knowing that she'd never want to reveal what had been pulled from her. She had to say the words out loud. Had to rip off her protective layer and show him the ugliness inside.

"I can't have kids."

"What?" he asked, his incredulous tone at odds with the anger in his face.

"I can't conceive," she said, hating to say the words. Always she'd hoped it wasn't true, that some sort of mistake had been made but her doctor's words of thirteen years ago still lingered in her mind, and she'd never wanted to hear them again.

Your chance of conceiving a child is so small to almost be nil.

"That's it—your big secret?"

"Yes. I know that a woman who can't have children is about as appealing as a sack of potatoes with heads sprouting on them. And it didn't matter as much with my ex-fiancé. I never loved him. But I love you, Luke. It feels sometimes as if I've loved you forever, and I absolutely hate the fact that I can't ever have a child because I want yours.'' Tears streamed down her face and she wiped them away with a brisk movement of her hand.

She looked at him expecting to see disgust or anger, instead finding his face devoid of any expression. Never before had she seen him that closed off, that cold. Oh, God, she'd killed any feelings he had for her. She knew that would happen.

''I'm sorry,'' she said quietly, and turned to walk out the door.

Thirteen

Luke grabbed Miranda's arm before she'd taken a step toward the door. He couldn't let her go like that. As if she'd never been anything more to him than a vessel to carry his children. He smiled despite the pain caused by Miranda's hurt. He'd never trusted women because they had the power to procreate and to lie about who they'd done so with, but here was a woman he could trust. Ah, hell, he already did.

"Miranda, darlin'. The fact that you can't have kids makes you more appealing."

She grimaced and tugged her arm out of his grip. "All men say it doesn't matter until they start thinking long-term and inevitably they all do. And then, you'll regret being tied to a woman who can't give you your place in history. A woman who can't let you pass on some part of yourself for generations."

Luke bit back an instinctive curse. What the hell kind of man had her ex-fiancé been? *Not much of one.* Not that he'd displayed any more tact by blurting out his questions.

What a mess. He'd been worried about her leaving him and now he knew why—he was never letting her go.

Luke pulled Miranda into his arms. "Hold still, darlin'. I'm not going to hurt you."

"Just let me go," she said, her voice cool and aloof.

He already had hurt her. The pain was evident in her voice. "Ah, babe."

"I've revealed more to you than I have to any man. I need some time to myself," she said, glancing up at him with her mist gray eyes. Only tonight the mist didn't seem peaceful and soothing. Tonight it was dismal and frightened.

He dropped his hands not wanting to inflict further injury to her soul. She walked stiffly to the fireplace and stared into the flames. Her sexy dress and sophisticated coif was at odds with the aura of fragility surrounding her. She seemed so alone—so lost.

Miranda pretended to be the ultimate ice princess when it came to emotions, but he knew better. She'd been wounded deeply by his comments and though he knew he should let her go before he became more deeply entangled in her life, he knew that he couldn't. It was too late....

She loved him.

The words hadn't seemed real before. Not one other person had ever said those words to him. Not his mother, who had died when he was very young. Not his father, whose respect he'd had at one point in his life and certainly not his ex-wife. But coming from Miranda, the words felt right. As if they belonged to him and her alone.

"Dammit, woman. I can't let you go."

He stalked over to her ready to shake her if need be to convince her of his sincerity. The fine trembling of her shoulders and the sheen of tears in her mist gray eyes betrayed her. His frustration drained out of him like air from a popped balloon. Coaxing her gently back into his arms, he held her tightly until she relaxed against him.

He'd never been good with words and had no idea what to say to heal her wounds. She hurt from more than his words, she had probably relived every harsh thing her ex-fiancé had said to her.

"Don't think about it."

"About what?"

"Whatever he said to you that made you feel like less than a woman."

She glared at him over her shoulder. "I don't feel like less than a woman."

"What do you feel like?"

"I don't know," she said shrugging. "Like there's something indefinable about me that turns men off."

He cursed savagely under his breath. Didn't she understand that simply being with her turned him on? That thinking about her laughter, her smile, her grit made him so hard his jeans fit tight. That being away from her caused his heart to ache in a way that the organ never had before.

He'd invited her into his home, his bed and his life. Showed her his craft of furniture making, his tattoo and his music. His most private and personal parts of his soul, he'd allowed her to glimpse and Miranda thought he didn't want her in his life anymore.

Miranda refused to meet his gaze, keeping her head tucked under his chin. He wanted to see her, to discern some of what she'd been thinking.

"Darlin', you couldn't turn me *off* if you tried."

She glanced up. "Really?"

"Have I ever lied to you?"

"No, you haven't." She snuggled closer to him. "It's just so hard to believe."

"Well, believe it."

"I do."

He held her in his arms until she started to yawn, then carried her up the stairs. He smiled at the sleepy way she cuddled closer to him. Hell, he was in trouble now—Miranda had crawled into his heart and he'd never be able to oust her.

For once the thought of being codependent on someone didn't create instinctive panic. His daddy's laughter didn't echo in his mind and Luke took heart from that. Possibly he'd made the right choice this time and found a woman he could love, respect and trust.

Miranda woke the next morning to the haunting sound of Luke's harmonica. She stretched hoping to find Luke nearby, but her hand encountered empty space. She was disappointed at being alone until she heard the instrument's soft cry greeting the morning and her. Its sensual lament stirred her emotions.

Rolling over she hugged his pillow to her chest, the soft cloth no match for the remembered strength of his arms around her all night.

Miranda followed the sound of the soul-wrenching music down the stairs. She trailed her fingers down the banister, loving the feel of the hardwood beneath her touch. She knew Luke had carved and created every piece of his house by hand.

The smell of coffee lingered in the air but didn't tempt her. She wanted to find Luke. The door to the back porch was open and she stepped outside. The mist lay heavily on the ground and filled the air with a sense of expectancy. The captivating sound of Luke's mouth harp made a counterpoint to the unsettling feeling. Sounding like a safe haven in the shrouded morning.

A cool breeze blew gently, stirring the mists and revealing Luke. He stood not more than ten feet away with his back toward her. He wore no shirt and faded jeans that rode low on his hips. A strong tendril of desire unfurled within her body.

Her body quickened with the need to be with Luke—to mate with him in a very primitive way. His music had done more than warm her soul, it had started a fire in her body that only his touch could extinguish.

The soft feel of his T-shirt against her skin made her realize that she was dressed inappropriately for this encounter. She should be wearing satin and lace. Something see-through and sexy, not his cast-off shirt. But satin and lace had never been her. Lace itched and satin made her feel as if she was going to slide off the bed.

Her first step off the porch felt the same as Alice's first step through the looking glass. She knew that she was stepping into a world familiar yet unfamiliar. She shivered but not with fear. Anticipation quivered in her body.

The cool grass under her feet served as a counterpoint to the heat in her veins. The mist surrounded her, urging her forward. She obeyed the mist and her body, stepping toward Luke. The hawk claimed her attention again seemingly drawing her closer, asking her to set it free.

Luke turned before she took another step, but continued playing. She closed the gap between them, staring into his deep brown eyes, seeing for the first time the depth of his caring revealed there. Reaching out she let her fingertips caress the muscled planes of his chest. She felt the song bubble up from inside of him.

The song ended on a high note. Miranda shook with the need to get closer to him. Gently she took the harmonica from him. Sliding her fingers along the seam of his lips, she stroked his mouth as his song had her soul.

"Did you like the song?" he asked. Each word he spoke brushed against her fingers.

"Yes," she said, her voice husky to her own ears.

He chuckled, a sexy, masculine sound that told her he knew what desires his music had stirred. He leaned back, glancing down her body, his gaze lingering on her breasts. Her nipples tightened in response. His smile widened.

He reached out to toy with her hardened flesh—the sensation no less arousing than his music had been.

He brought his other hand up under her T-shirt and Miranda felt as if she'd been tossed into a fierce storm. The heat and swirling emotions were fighting for dominance in her body. She clung to him, nails digging into his shoulders as the tension gathered in her center.

"Ah, darlin', that's it. Let me feel your passion."

She wanted to do more than show him her passion. She needed to experience his passion, as well. She bent, kissing his flat nipple. His grip on her paused ever so slightly before resuming.

Using her fingers and mouth she caressed every inch of his torso. She'd never cared about a man's desires before, but suddenly she wanted to fulfill all of Luke's.

She stopped at the waistband of his jeans, gathering the courage to go on. A quick glance at Luke showed eager anticipation.

"I don't think we're evenly dressed," she said as she unbuttoned his denims. She reached into the opening created and stroked the hot length of him. He groaned low in his throat.

He grabbed the hem of her shirt and ripped the garment from her body. Lifting her with his hands on her waist he brought her breasts level with his mouth and greedily suckled there. The feeling was so intense she forgot to breathe.

She needed to be closer to him. She needed to have his hands on her body, his mouth on hers and his body driving steadily into her own.

"Wrap your legs around my waist," he said, his voice low, sounding almost guttural.

She complied at once, pushing the rough fabric of his jeans out of the way first. She thrilled at the close contact, the flesh-to-flesh connection that her body, soul, heart had been craving for an entire lifetime.

The silky, smooth feeling of his masculine flesh threw her off guard for a second. Luke had never made love to her without using a condom.

He kissed his way up her chest to her neck and finally took her mouth in a deep kiss that left her feeling completely weakened.

"I'm sorry, darlin', I can't wait."

"What about protection?"

He froze, his passion-filled eyes staring down into hers. She knew that his control hung by a tenuous thread. She felt the pulse of his life pressed against her most private flesh.

"No, I want to feel your flesh on mine. Nothing between us except the morning mist."

She reached up twining her fingers in the hair at the nape of his neck as he thrust into her. Their joining was quick and hot, setting her senses on fire. Never before had she made love with a man who knew and accepted all of her secrets. Miranda felt her soul bond with Luke, she felt a melding of two distinct and separate beings into one.

They found completion as one and sank to the ground as strength left them both. Luke held her wrapped in his arms, so closely that she felt he'd never let go. She hoped he'd never let go.

Fourteen

Miranda frowned at the computer screen and stood up. She'd felt queasy and tired for the past week and a half. At first, she'd written off her malady as nerves due to starting her freelance career. She'd begun to wonder if it wasn't the flu.

Over the past month since her confession, he'd opened up and begun to share more of his life. She smiled to herself, for the first time happy that she couldn't actually get pregnant. She still had hopes of convincing him someday to marry her and adopt a child. But he didn't want to talk about the future, only the eternal present, which bothered her.

She forced herself to sit back down at her desk. Her career as a freelance business consultant might be short-lived if she didn't learn how to concentrate. Unfortunately, she saw Luke through the bank of windows. He'd moved his workbench outside and stood shirtless, working on an intricate design for a cabinet door. Maybe when he was finished, they could share a bath outside or go for a ride on his Harley. She tingled with the memory of the sun setting around them as she welcomed him into her body.

Luke was coming to trust her more and more. He still used condoms most of the time when he made love to her, but in the middle of the night, he sometimes reached for her and made love to her with an intensity that made her shiver to remember it. At those times, he forgot his inherent caution and that gave her hope that he might care for her more than he wanted to admit even to himself.

A few minutes later, she heard Luke's steps on the front porch. She saved the spreadsheet she'd been working with.

"Want to grab lunch in town?" he asked as he came in the front door.

"Sure. Are you ready to go?" she asked. His long hair held back in a ponytail gave him that rebel look she loved so well. Sweat glistened on his upper torso and she wanted him with an intensity that left her breathless.

"Yeah, give me a minute to wash up," he said, crossing to her. He bent and kissed her. She stood, wrapping her arms around his waist. His scent surrounded her, earthy, masculine and so tempting that she tasted the flesh of his shoulder. Here was the cure for the muggy feeling that had been plaguing her all morning, she thought.

She loved the feel of those strong muscles against her breasts. She wished he didn't have an appointment in town. But he did. He stepped back after long minutes had passed.

"Are you feeling better, darlin'?" he asked, his drawling tone brushing over aroused senses.

"A bit. I plan to stop into the drugstore while we're in town. I think it might be some sort of stomach flu."

"Must be from eating your own cooking."

Luke chuckled and wrapped an arm around her shoulders, leading her to the stairs. Miranda gave him a look of reprimand.

"I thought you said I was improving." It was embarrassing to be so lacking in the domestic arts but she'd never taken the time to really learn how to cook. Last night's dinner hadn't been burned at all, which she thought was a step in the right direction.

"Darlin', you've got no way to go but up, but you're still a long way from cordon bleu trained."

He dropped another quick kiss on her lips and went up the stairs to shower and change. Miranda went back to the computer and continued working on the business plan she'd been paid to put together for a new project the Jessup Springs resort was thinking of starting.

A strong breeze blew through the open windows and Miranda wrinkled her nose at the pungent scent. She felt her throat begin to close and gagged at the smell. Her stomach heaved. She stood and ran to the downstairs bathroom, barely making it to the toilet before her breakfast came up.

Without really thinking about, she reached out and closed the bathroom door. She definitely didn't want Luke to see her like this. She needed to buy a new cookbook if it was her cooking making her sick.

Then with a sudden spark of humor, she remembered that Luke had fixed the morning meal.

She washed her face and left the bathroom. Luke was halfway down the stairs when she reentered the room. He stopped and looked at her with concern in his deep brown eyes.

"You okay?"

"Yes, I'm fine."

"Are you sure?" he asked, obviously concerned.

She nodded, afraid to speak because his care touched her more than she'd ever imagined it would. No use bothering him with her illness.

Luke waited in the crowded diner for Miranda. He glanced at his watch. How long could it take to buy a package of antacid tablets?

Miranda entered a few minutes later with a large bag and made her way through the luncheon crowd toward him. She still looked pale and her eyes had a strange expression in them, but she smiled when she saw him. Luke still wasn't used to the feelings she generated in him. It was like taking a punch to the heart. The organ stopped beating for a frozen second then began again.

He stood when she approached the booth and waited until she sat down before seating himself again. The hovering waitress took their order and then left. Miranda toyed with her water glass almost nervously.

"What did the pharmacist say?" Luke asked at last, knowing that she wasn't going to talk about whatever illness she might have.

"Not much. I'm not sure he's too reliable," she said, fiddling with her silverware.

"Why?" he asked, sitting back when the waitress dropped off their salads.

Miranda picked at hers before answering him. "He's kind of old and hasn't been to any seminars in the past five years. The medical world changes quite frequently."

"James would never steer you wrong. What did he think was wrong with you? Did you mention that your cooking could be to blame?"

"Yes. He suggested that I try one or two herbal remedies and if the symptoms persist to go see the doctor. How did your appointment go?"

He told her about his new job, realizing for the first time how nice it was to share the mundane details of his business and life with someone. He'd never exchanged small-time chitchat with someone who was important. Actually, he didn't think there was another person who'd cared about those details of his life.

Luke let the buzz of nearby conversation settle around them like a warm blanket on a cold day. He and Miranda were wrapped in a cocoon of their own making. He felt

more than content. He felt at peace with his world for the
first time.

Miranda had waited until she was sure Luke had gone
outside to his workshop before sneaking out of the bed the
next morning. The hardwood floor was cold against her
feet, but she shivered more from anxiety than from cold.
She picked up Luke's discarded shirt and wrapped it around
her naked body as she continued into the bathroom.

The pharmacist said that her symptoms were indicative
of only one thing—pregnancy. A quick call to her own
doctor when she'd arrived home had yielded results that
made her stomach churn but with fear not nausea. Her one
remaining ovary, even with a scarred fallopian tube gave
her a ten percent chance of conceiving. She wished Dr.
Franklin had been as forthcoming when she'd been a young
girl so she wouldn't have spent her entire life feeling in-
complete.

Dr. Franklin said her mother had felt that a slim chance
wasn't worth mentioning. Her father had wanted to encourage Miranda to use her intelligence to go farther in the
business field than her sister who had a hundred percent
chance of conceiving and bearing children.

The three tests she'd purchased all had similar instructions and she followed them closely not wanting to take
any chances. Oh, God, she thought as she stared at her
watch, waiting for the allotted amount of time to pass. *What
if I am pregnant?*

After years of believing that she could never be, the possibility scared and thrilled her. Luke would never believe
that she hadn't betrayed him. She could just not tell him,
but eventually he'd notice that she was putting on weight....

The loud pounding on the bathroom door startled her.
She grabbed her throat. Her heart thudded so strongly she
felt as if it might burst from her chest. Stars danced in front
of her eyes, she feared she'd pass out.

"Darlin', you okay?" Luke asked, his voice strong and sure. There was never any doubt in him.

"Uh, yes. I'm doing one of those female things, so I'll be out in a little while."

"Another mud facial?" he asked.

She heard the laughter in his voice and remembered the last time she'd locked herself in the bathroom. Luke had insisted on seeing her with the facial pack on and somehow he'd turned what could have been an extremely embarrassing moment into an erotic one. They'd ended up with mud all over each other and the bed by the time they were finished.

"No," she said at last. She definitely didn't want him joining her.

"When will you be out?"

She checked her watch. "One minute, thirty seconds."

"Great, I'm fixing breakfast so don't waste time."

She heard him retreat and turned back to the three innocuous-looking contraptions. They held her future in their inanimate hands. She didn't know if she could look. Two minutes passed and still she sat staring at the pregnancy tests.

Finally she stood and looked. It took about twenty seconds to register that she was indeed pregnant according to the first test. She double-checked the box and then the wand again. The other two were positive, as well.

Miranda didn't know what to do. She couldn't run down the stairs and share her news with Luke. She hugged herself, unable to believe that she'd have her chance at motherhood after all. *Probably single-motherhood.* Shivers coursed through her body, and she shook when she reached for the door handle. She sat down on the closed lid of the toilet.

Maybe he'd understand when she explained. Maybe he'd realize that she wasn't trying to trap him. Maybe he'd accept the miracle their love had given them. But years in the business world had taught her that harsh reality more often than not ruled the day.

She left the bathroom and dressed quickly in jeans and a T-shirt before going downstairs.

Luke had set out their places at the kitchen table. But she couldn't sit down. Nervously she cleared her throat. He faced her, carrying bowls of fresh fruit to the table.

"This should be better than your cooking and might help your stomach problems," he said.

Her throat closed against threatening tears at his kindness. As much as she'd always wished she could have a child, she now wished she didn't have to tell him that they'd conceived a child after she'd told him she was infertile.

"I don't think it was my cooking," she said carefully after he'd lowered the bowls to the table.

"What do you think it was?" he asked, concern evident in his tone.

"The fact that I'm…pregnant."

"What?!" He staggered backward as if from a physical blow.

"I'm pregnant," she repeated, though she knew he'd heard her. "I doubted it myself, but we'll have to accept that a miracle has happened."

"There's no such thing as a miracle," he said harshly. He plowed his fingers through his hair and rocked back on his heels. She couldn't read all the emotions on his face. Shock, anger and something else…something almost like betrayal.

Miranda realized suddenly that Luke didn't trust her and probably never had. It explained so much that she'd been willing to overlook before. She understood why an open-ended, noncommitted relationship worked best for Luke. It was all he had to give to a woman. No woman could make up for the brutal lesson his ex-wife and brother had taught him.

"What really happened to you? I thought you were barren."

"You don't understand, I had a cyst on my ovary when I was sixteen and it was removed," she said, trying to explain to him what still seemed shockingly unreal to her.

"Does that mean you have no eggs?"

"No, I still have one ovary but the fallopian tube was scarred and blocked. There was a ten percent chance that I could conceive, but my parents apparently decided that the slim percentage wasn't worth mentioning to me."

He didn't say anything, only stared at her as if she'd grown two heads. She knew he'd need time to come to terms with all that she'd told him. She'd probably finished the job his ex-wife had done on him.

"I think I'll move back to my rental cabin," she said, hoping that a bit of distance would help him understand she hadn't betrayed him.

"Maybe you should return to Atlanta. You probably need to go to your doctor."

Miranda fought the urge not to cry. He wanted her not only out of his house, but off his mountain and back in a place where he'd never want to live. He wasn't just thinking of the temporary separation she'd been hoping for. He wanted her out of his life forever.

Luke pivoted and stalked to the front door.

"I'll pack and get out of here today. Luke?"

He glanced back over his shoulder not saying another word.

"I didn't betray your trust," she said softly.

He continued out the door and only the harsh echo of the slamming door answered her. She wrapped her arms around her waist trying to hold everything inside. But she couldn't. Hot tears fell down her face and she knew that she'd never see Luke Romero again.

Fifteen

Two weeks had passed since Miranda's shocking an nouncement. Luke had followed her into town on the Har ley to ensure that she made it safely off of his mountain.

He'd stopped off at a small bar with the intention o getting drunk, but he didn't want to dull the pain of he announcement. He needed to wallow in it, to accept tha she was no longer a part of his life, to acknowledge once again that he'd misjudged a woman, to admit to himsel that Miranda was really gone.

So instead he'd driven recklessly through the winding foothills of his mountain on the motorcycle. Challenging the road with careless abandon, trying not to think abou her. But it was impossible....

He missed her.

Luke stared at the meadow where he'd first seen Mir anda. She'd looked up at him from those wild curls of her and he'd been lost. The flowers were fading in his garde and the woods looked harsh and uncompromising in th deepening twilight. Much the same as it must have seemed to Miranda her first night on the mountain. He remembered the intriguing blend of "real" woman and "city" sophistication. That ridiculous bag of junk food she'd toted everywhere.

He left the porch and went to stand in the middle of the field that was his backyard. He remembered the cold morning mist and Miranda's hot passion as she surrounded him. Offering herself to the man she loved without any protection or barriers, just the honesty of desire and lovemaking flesh upon flesh.

He realized that their early morning bonding had been so much more than the familiarity of lovers reaching for each other in mutual need. It had been a bonding of wounded souls, an event to set in motion a healing process in both of them. It had been the moment he'd first acknowledged to himself that he loved her.

But a baby. He didn't want to leave himself that vulnerable again. He'd loved Brett with every bit of his soul, and losing him had been the final straw in an already dismal situation. Would Miranda betray him that way? Let him love another child only to take the child away from him?

Confused and angry, he'd lashed out when she told him. The anger not directed at Miranda but at himself for allowing her to slip past his guard. There was something about Miranda's blend of sophistication and innocence that caught him unawares.

Only she wasn't innocent any longer.

Damn, he'd trusted her. Though he didn't believe she knowingly betrayed him. She'd violated his trust just the same.

I told you not to trust her, his daddy's voice echoed in his ears, mocking him.

Suddenly another voice echoed in his mind. Miranda's. *I didn't betray your trust.*

Her last words hadn't bothered him at the time because

he'd been too angry to really hear them, but now they haunted him when he least expected it.

She'd trusted him, too. Revealed things about herself that she'd never shared with another man. He couldn't help the possessiveness, the rightness he felt when he remembered the first moment his body had entered hers. Miranda was all that was good and kind and he was, he thought with bitter regret, all that was destructive.

As betrayed as he'd felt, Miranda must feel that more so. Her miracle after years of despair and heartache had spelled the end to their relationship and she knew it. That was why tears had shined in her eyes and her voice had sounded cracked and fragile like an old woman's.

He'd betrayed her trust in him.

A baby.

He still couldn't believe it. His own child, growing in Miranda's small, curvy body made desire course through his veins. The body he'd come to know so well in such a short time. A being that was both him and her. God, he hoped the baby was more Miranda because he had more flaws than a corrupt televangelist.

A miracle.

What type of father would he be? The same kind his dad had been? What if he failed the child in the same way his father had failed him? Irrevocably breaking the bonds of family until nothing would repair them? *Nothing except the love of a good woman.*

Miranda would be the balance that made everything all right, he realized suddenly. She'd be there for him and their child in a way his mother never had. His mother had died when he was six months old. *Probably baking burnt cookies.*

He didn't want to have a child with anyone else. Because with someone else there was the chance that he'd louse it up and hurt the child. But Miranda believed in him, centered him...and he'd driven her away.

He grabbed his keys and left the cabin. He needed to get her back. He needed to tell her that he loved her. He needed to make her understand that when she'd walked out the door, she'd taken his soul with her.

But first he needed to reconcile his past. To make some sense of what happened with Suzanne and Jake. If Jake felt a tenth of what Luke felt for Miranda then he understood why his brother had been unable to stay away from Suzanne.

He let go of the bitterness and betrayal he'd been clinging to in order to keep from falling in love again. To keep from moving on into the future—a future that wouldn't be complete without Miranda. He couldn't have both, he realized. He couldn't have the future he wanted without saying goodbye to the past.

Lifting a cigar to his mouth, he lit it and toasted his father and brother silently. Without their valuable lessons in family struggle and betrayal he would never have met Miranda, and that was one thing he wouldn't have missed for the whole world.

Miranda morosely took another Mallomar from the package, trying not to think about the fact that she'd eaten almost the whole thing. Her condo seemed cold and lonely on the early fall evening. Twilight cast long shadows around the room, which suited her mood.

She'd quit her job after negotiating benefits coverage throughout her pregnancy. She planned to continue her freelance consulting firm. The fast pace of the city left her feeling lethargic which her doctor assured was a direct effect of her pregnancy. In fact, even Atlanta seemed too busy, too crowded, too much especially now that she was thinking of the future and raising her baby in this environment.

She missed the mountains and had, with that thought in mind, made arrangements to rent an office in Asheville. Her

parents were driving to North Carolina with her next week
to help her find a house to move into. She wanted every
detail in place before the baby arrived.

She longed for the quiet morning mists that ringed
Luke's mountain. She wanted to enjoy the slow-paced city
of Jessup Springs where no one really hurried unless something was on fire. The homey family feeling that she got
sitting on the bench outside the town's only diner. At the
same time she longed to experience the serenity of waking
in the arms of the man she loved.

She missed Luke. She wanted him to share the feelings
of accomplishment and wonder that the baby growing inside her brought.

It was ridiculous in the face of the fact that he'd told her
to leave, to get off his mountain and far away from him.
The fact that he believed she'd betrayed him in a way no
other woman had before; not by getting pregnant, because
Luke would take responsibility for the child, she knew it
with the same bone-deep certainty that she knew he
couldn't face the future with her and their child. But by not
being what he'd expected.

She'd gone to visit her doctor and he'd assured her she
was pregnant and everything was proceeding normally. Her
mother was excited about the fact that Miranda was going
to be a mother. Her father still had problems with the fact
that she was a single mom, but he'd been secretly pleased.

The condo was clean and neat. Before sitting down with
the box of cookies, she'd had a cleaning fit and dusted the
entire house. She reached for the glass of milk and grimaced at the empty bottom of the cup. She didn't really
want to get up and go into the kitchen.

Reluctantly she went and refilled her glass. On her way
back to the living room she scrutinized her town house.
The antiques she'd taken the time to collect and refinish
filled every inch of living space, but the place still remained
lonely. She hoped it would be better in her new place when

her child was born. But her pregnancy had the surreal quality of a Hollywood movie set. Real but not really. After years of expecting her career and material possessions to be her only legacy, this child...

Miranda felt the prickle of tears that came so easily lately. She really had to get over all this weeping. Thoughts of her new baby and thoughts of Luke brought an onslaught that no effort could control.

True, she'd never been in love before but her feelings were spiraling from anger to sympathy to remorse that he couldn't be all she'd expected him to be. All that she sensed lying just under the surface of his inner wall. She sank to the sofa after taking a deep breath.

The doorbell chimed and she surreptitiously wiped her eyes as she made her way to the door. It was probably her sister, Fay, with another maternity book. Fay had three children and had been mothering Miranda since she'd returned home.

The doorbell chimed again. She sensed the impatience of the person on the other side. Definitely not Fay.

"Who is it?" she asked, without opening the door.

"Luke Romero, darlin'. Open up."

She staggered backward, wondering what he was doing there. Then she decided she didn't really want to know. What if he'd come to heap more accusations on her head? What if he'd come to claim her child and not her?

"Go away," she said, her voice broke. *Why was he here?*

"Let me in, Miranda," he said. His deep voice brought a rush of memories with it. Memories of the two of them in his loft bedroom, the clear starry night and full moon bathing their naked bodies in faint light. Memories of his mouth moving on the harmonica, playing songs that made her soul weep. Memories of him turning his back on her and telling her to leave.

"No." She walked away from the door, ignoring the

sounds of his pounding on the hardwood surface and repeatedly ringing the doorbell.

She returned to the living room, picking up her cookies and glass of milk. How dare he come here after he'd told her to get out his life? How dare he remind her of how much he'd meant to her? How was she ever going to get over him?

"Miranda, open this door." She heard his voice like a boom of thunder echoing through her quiet house. She panicked, knowing that she was in no mood to deal with him rationally. Maybe in a couple of weeks she'd send him a letter, inviting him to call her. But not tonight. She'd heard the baby's heartbeat for the first time today and she wanted to share that with Luke. Not this Luke, the one he'd been before she'd told him she was expecting.

Instead of going to let him in, she turned on her CD player and turned the volume up until she was sure the neighbors could hear the strains of the *William Tell* Overture.

She went back to the foyer, listening carefully and not hearing a single sound. Luke had left. She felt a wave of sadness wash over her. Obviously he hadn't been that determined to talk to her.

The sudden silence in the wake of the booming overture alerted her that someone else was in the house with her. The sound of footsteps behind her made her pivot on her heel. Standing in the faint light spilling from the living room was Luke. He calmly replaced some tools in a small leather pouch, stuffing it in his back pocket.

In the light spilling from the living room, he looked as wild, decadent and pagan as he had on the night they'd met. His long hair was pulled back revealing the twinkling diamond stud earring. He wore indecently tight jeans and those battered boots of his. The tight black T-shirt revealed his strength and Miranda had never felt weaker than she did at that moment.

"How did you get in here?" she asked.

"Through the back door. I shut the CD player off before one of your neighbors calls the cops."

"Maybe I'll call them to arrest the intruder in my house."

"You know you're safe with me."

Yeah, right, she thought. Safe from physical harm, but emotionally...there was only so much one woman could take and Miranda knew her threshold was near.

"Convince me not to call the police," she said.

He strode forward like a bold marauder from times past—like the outlaw he essentially was. Miranda had the feeling that she'd pushed him past the limits of his self-control.

The door blocked her retreat. Though she knew he wouldn't hurt her, his anger was palpable. She reached behind her, trying to open the dead bolt and door handle. Just as she sprung the lock on the door, Luke lunged forward and scooped her up.

"Forget it," he growled. "Your running days are over, darlin'."

"No."

"Yes," he said firmly.

She'd always known he was stronger than she was, but had never resented that strength until now. She couldn't deal with Luke tonight. Not after she'd just finished a whole box of Mallomars and drank enough milk to float a battleship.

"Can we talk later? I'm not really up to company tonight."

"No."

Luke, the great conversationalist. To think she once thought country charm beat city sophistication. Then again, she still did. That was why the ache of missing Luke hadn't ceased.

He carried her into the living room and plunked her on

the couch. He stood in the doorway an immovable barrier between her and emotional security. His expression was more determined.

Her arms ached with the need to wrap herself around him. She'd thought she'd forgotten how he could set her pulse racing and her hormones on fire, but one brief contact and she was shaking.

What did he want? She wondered if he'd try to take the baby from her. Maybe he wanted to have visitation rights to the child. Maybe, she thought with more hope than common sense, he wanted to be with her and the baby.

"Why are you here, Luke?" she asked.

Silence met her question and though she really wouldn't call the cops on him, she crossed to the phone and picked up the earpiece. Glancing at him, she waited.

"You're not going to call the cops and we both know it."

"You're right, but I think after all that determination to get inside you'd want to tell me what's on your mind. I really don't want to play games with you tonight."

"Dammit, darlin', I'm not playing a game."

"Then why are you here?"

"Because you're not on my mountain."

"You told me to leave, remember?"

"I've regretted it. Nothing's the same since you've gone. And I realized that it won't be the same unless you come back."

"Why the sudden change of heart?"

"I just needed some time to come to terms with everything. Your announcement was so sudden."

"You thought I'd betrayed you."

He rushed over to her. He reached out to touch her but froze before his hand made contact with her. She stared at his strong tanned hand. A hand that evoked fire in her body, tenderness in her heart and aching in her soul when he used it to play his harmonica.

"You'd never betray me. You couldn't."

She shook her head, not really understanding what he was saying.

"You called our baby a miracle and I thought it was a mistake, but I've realized that it wasn't a miracle that helped us to conceive that child, Miranda."

"What was it?"

"It was you. Your love unlocked the frozen part of my soul. You were the miracle, not the baby."

"Oh, Luke," she said softly, unable to stop the tears falling slowly down her face.

"If it's not too late, I want you back in my life and on my mountain."

"Why?"

"Because I love you."

Miranda closed the gap between them, wrapping her arms around Luke. He held her so tightly she could hardly breathe, but that didn't matter. She wiped her wet face against his shirtfront and heard his breath break.

"I was so afraid I'd lost you," he said quietly.

"Never," she said. "I kept trying to get over you but you wouldn't leave my heart."

"I had the same difficulty but my mule-headedness got in the way."

"I wish it hadn't."

"Me, too, especially seeing all the junk food you've been eating."

"I figured it was safer for the baby than my cooking."

Luke laughed and watched her eyes darken. He'd made the right decision in coming to find her, as if he could have done anything else.

"I'll take care of the both of you from now on."

She smiled up at Luke, knowing that he would take excellent care of them both.

Epilogue

A mountain of white frothy bubbles covered the entire surface of the old-fashioned claw-foot bathtub. The foamy spray beckoned Luke closer and he stripped off his clothes as he walked forward. Where was his little minx of a wife?

Their six-month-old daughter, Jenny, was spending the night in town with her grandparents, giving Luke and Miranda some time to themselves. Though he doted on his daughter and loved her more than he'd thought possible, he was looking forward to being alone with Miranda.

The setting sun cast long shadows on the grass and wildflowers that blanketed the lawn. Luke wanted to tilt his head back and emit a rebel yell.

As he watched, the bubbles parted and a head emerged amid a spray of steam and foam. Dark curly locks brushed against a curvy back with a small rosebud tattoo. The tattoo that she'd insisted he draw for her. It reflected so many changes in his wife. His fingers tingled with the need to trace the design and the smooth line of her spine.

He cleared his throat hoping to catch her attention, but the sound died before it reached his lips.

She shook her head flinging soap and water everywhere, stretching her arms toward the sky as if to embrace the night. Her breasts thrust upward, their large aureoles begging for his caress. Luke shed the last of his clothing and stood above her.

"Darlin'," he growled.

"It's about time you got home," she said. Her eyes widened as she took in his unclothed aroused state.

"Want to join me?"

"What do you think?"

She shifted her slim legs to make room for him and he slid into the tub facing her.

"Turn around and lean against me," he said.

"Wait."

She reached over the side of the tub and brought a cigar. He lifted one eyebrow in question but she only smiled her mysterious smile. The one that made him want to take her hard, deep and fast.

She clipped the crown of the cigar and picked up the butane lighter. Running the flame up and down the length of the cigar as he'd taught her to, she winked at him.

"Open up," she said.

He did and she placed the cigar in his mouth and lit the end. She made sure the entire end of the cigar was lit. Then produced a snifter of brandy. As he puffed on the cigar, she removed it from his mouth and held the glass up.

He took a sip and watched his wife enjoy his cigar as much as he ever had. He tilted his head back and let out a loud rebel yell. Ready to stake a claim.

He picked up his battered Stetson. Smoke drifted upward in a lazy spiral, merging with the clouds of steam. He settled the hat low on Miranda's head and removed the cigar from her lips.

He set it on the deck next to the brandy snifter and drew

her to him. She settled on his lap, facing him, and he took her the way he'd dreamed of: hard, fast and deep.

The satisfaction they took in each other's bodies rocked him to the foundation of his soul. He settled her against his chest and let the evening come alive around them. Luke felt at long last that they'd both come home and found their place in life.

* * * * *

Take 2 bestselling love stories FREE

Plus get a FREE surprise gift!

Special Limited-Time Offer

Mail to Silhouette Reader Service™

3010 Walden Avenue
P.O. Box 1867
Buffalo, N.Y. 14240-1867

YES! Please send me 2 free Silhouette Desire® novels and my free surprise gift. Then send me 6 brand-new novels every month, which I will receive months before they appear in bookstores. Bill me at the low price of $3.12 each plus 25¢ delivery and applicable sales tax, if any.* That's the complete price, and a saving of over 10% off the cover prices—quite a bargain! I understand that accepting the books and gift places me under no obligation ever to buy any books. I can always return a shipment and cancel at any time. Even if I never buy another book from Silhouette, the 2 free books and the surprise gift are mine to keep forever.

225 SEN CH7U

Name	(PLEASE PRINT)	
Address	Apt. No.	
City	State	Zip

This offer is limited to one order per household and not valid to present Silhouette Desire® subscribers. *Terms and prices are subject to change without notice.
Sales tax applicable in N.Y.

UDES-98 ©1990 Harlequin Enterprises Limited

#1 *New York Times* bestselling author

NORA ROBERTS

Presents a brand-new book in the beloved MacGregor series:

THE WINNING HAND
(SSE#1202)

October 1998 in

Silhouette®SPECIAL EDITION®

Innocent Darcy Wallace needs Mac Blade's protection in the high-stakes world she's entered. But who will protect Mac from the irresistible allure of this vulnerable beauty?

**Coming in March, the much-anticipated novel,
THE MacGREGOR GROOMS
Also, watch for the MacGregor stories
where it all began!**

**December 1998:
THE MacGREGORS: Serena—Caine**

**February 1999:
THE MacGREGORS: Alan—Grant**

**April 1999:
THE MacGREGORS: Daniel—Ian**

Available at your favorite retail outlet, only from

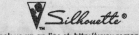

INTIMATE MOMENTS®

™ *Silhouette*®

**Coming in October from
Silhouette Intimate Moments...**

BRIDES OF THE NIGHT

Silhouette Intimate Moments fulfills your wildest
wishes in this compelling new in-line collection
featuring two very memorable men...tantalizing,
irresistible men who exist only in the darkness
but who hunger for the light of true love.

TWILIGHT VOWS
by Maggie Shayne

The unforgettable WINGS IN THE NIGHT miniseries
continues with a vampire hero to die for and the
lovely mortal woman who will go to any lengths to
save their unexpected love.

MARRIED BY DAWN
by Marilyn Tracy

Twelve hours was all the time this rogue vampire
had to protect an innocent woman. But was
marriage his only choice to keep her safe—if not
from the night...then from himself?

*Look for **BRIDES OF THE NIGHT** this October,
wherever Silhouette books are sold.*

™ *Silhouette*®

Look us up on-line at: http://www.romance.net   SIMBON

SILHOUETTE® *Desire*

COMING NEXT MONTH

#1171 THE LIONESS TAMER—Rebecca Brandewyne
Corporate tycoon Jordan Westcott, October's *Man of the Month,* gave up his reign as King of the Cement Jungle for a *real* challenge—taming the virginal spitfire Mistral St. Michel. But once this magnificent stranger transformed Mistral's fierce roar into a velvet purr would he find *himself* coming out of the wilderness...and spending a lifetime in this lioness's den?

#1172 THE LONE RIDER TAKES A BRIDE—Leanne Banks
The Rulebreakers

Rebellious Ben Palmer traveled through life fast and *alone*. So he'd certainly never get involved with adventureless Amelia Russell. What would Miss Straight and Narrow do with windblown hair, skirt flying up above her knees, traveling by the light of the full midnight moon? Well, it might just be worth a spin around the block to find out....

#1173 THE PATERNITY FACTOR—Caroline Cross
Wide-eyed beauty Jessy Ross had secretly loved the intense and sexy Shane Wyatt for years. Now she was sharing his home and caring for his baby—*a baby he'd discovered wasn't his.* He had vowed never to trust another woman as long as he lived. But Jessy had made her *own* solemn promise. To get to the bottom of Shane's bitterness—then get her man.

#1174 THE NON-COMMISSIONED BABY—Maureen Child
The Bachelor Battalion

Assignment: Fatherhood. Captain Jeff Ryan had just landed his toughest duty ever—daddy to a six-month-old baby girl. The valiant soldier enlisted expert help in the form of Laura Morgan...and *her* lovely form could stop a battleship. But could it anchor the heart of one tough marine?

#1175 THE OUTLAW'S WIFE—Cindy Gerard
Outlaw Hearts

Headstrong Emma James was tired of playing happy little homemaker to a "disinterested" husband. But the last thing Garrett wanted to lose was his beloved wife. So, even if it meant tying her up and toting her off, he'd show his feisty wife exactly how he felt about her—outlaw style!

#1176 COWBOYS, BABIES AND SHOTGUN VOWS—Shirley Rogers
Women To Watch

No woman had ever walked out on Ryder McCall! Outrage sent the proud cowboy chasing after one-night lover Ashley Bennett—but he wasn't expecting that *she'd* be expecting. Ryder wanted to be a real father—*and* husband. Could he convert Ashley's flat "no way" to a willing "I do"?